Everything around him faded away as he fell under the spell of watching her.

She twisted in the saddle and jabbed her index finger into the brim to tilt the hat away from her eyes.

Those eyes…

"Something wrong back there?"

Ryan shifted in the saddle and raised his head as if he'd been searching the ground the whole time. "Everything looks fine."

"Does it?"

He glanced at her and caught the look she gave him and, again, that amused smile. He cleared his throat. "Cody and Ty probably have a lot to report." He leaned forward and squinted at the ground, looking for footprints, dung, marks of passage, anything that would mean he wouldn't have to look at her. To his dismay, he could feel the heat of a blush on the back of his neck.

"I think you're cute, too."

Her words snapped him upright. She appeared innocent sitting astride her horse. But that smile was back, and now she was laughing.

"I—" He cleared his throat to loosen the words wedged there.

"Right." She faced forward, the words falling over her shoulder. "You keep looking for signs. I'll ride ahead."

And with that, Olivia Sattler poked her horse in the sides with her boots and left him stewing in the Wyoming sun—and suffocating in the cloud of dust kicked up by her horse's hooves.

S. DIONNE MOORE

is a multi-published author who makes her home in Pennsylvania with her husband of twenty-one years and her daughter. You can visit her at www.sdionnemoore.com.

Books by S. Dionne Moore

HEARTSONG PRESENTS

The Cattle Baron's Daughter

S. Dionne Moore

Heartsong Presents

To the heroes of the West, who stood their ground and believed in the dream of home, land, family, and peace.

A note from the Author:

I love to hear from my readers! You may correspond with me by writing:

S. Dionne Moore
Author Relations
P.O. Box 9048
Buffalo, NY 14240-9048

ISBN-13: 978-0-373-48615-1

THE CATTLE BARON'S DAUGHTER

This edition issued by special arrangement with Barbour Publishing, Inc., 1810 Barbour Drive, Uhrichsville, Ohio, U.S.A.

Chapter 1

The jingle of spurs punctuated his every footfall. Ryan Laxalt knew almost no one in Buffalo, Wyoming, though he knew his name would spark controversy and trouble. A man stepped from the stagecoach office and spat on the ground. When he raised his head and saw Ryan he nodded and swiped a hand across his lips. "If'n you're here to pick up someone, settle in. The stage should be here shortly. Name's Ronald P. Coltrain."

"Looking for information," Ryan said.

Ronald's eyes narrowed, and his gaze swept Ryan from head to foot. "You the law?"

"No."

"Then I ain't got nothing worth saying."

Ryan kept his hands loose at his sides, where his tied-down guns showed much about the manner of man he'd become in his long absence from Buffalo. "You might wish you'd talked."

Ronald licked his lips. "Stage is coming in. I've got work to do."

With a nod, Ryan swung away and retraced his steps. He should have expected as much. Few men wanted to snitch on another.

He leaned against a post support and squinted up and down Main Street. Strange, this street. What person would lay out a town's main road with a bend in it so you couldn't see straight from one end to the other unless you stood in the middle? His mother and father had chosen Johnson County as a place to settle and raise cattle. The town of Buffalo had come along later. Ryan remembered little of the actual town, though his travels had brought him to the Big Horn region once or twice. He'd left to make his own way as a foolish teen. He shook his head and used the heel of his boot to scratch the calf of his other leg. Back then he'd thought he had better methods of earning money, bigger dreams than working hard all day as his father had. Now, remorse at his arrogance stabbed guilt into his gut. The world had made quick work of shattering his idealistic thoughts.

Ronald popped his head out of the stage office and froze in place. He tilted his head as if listening. At first Ryan heard nothing; then the rattle of traces and the snap of a whip accompanied the distant rumble of horse hooves. He waited and watched as the driver brought the rig to a stop. A plume of dust lifted and spread, encompassing the coach. The driver sprang from the seat as if it were on fire then relaxed against the boot and rolled a smoke as the stage door swung outward. A tall form moved from the shadows of the interior and filled the narrow door. The man turned sideways to accommodate the width of his shoulders. By Ryan's eye, the man was an easterner. Fancy dress, a vest—rumpled but not looking too much like a man who'd come a far piece in the torturous interior of a hot stagecoach. He supposed the stranger would be a handsome man by a woman's standards, though to Ryan's way of thinking, he was far more fastidious than any man should be.

Behind him a door slapped into its frame, and a rounded woman wearing a dirty apron hurried by him. Other townspeople gathered, too, excited at the prospect of someone new coming to town, and probably even more curious because the man was so well dressed.

Ryan recognized only one face, and age had laid crags and sprouted more than a few gray hairs on the head of Papa Don, owner of the store. Most of the rest were too young for him to recall their faces.

The fancy man smacked dust from the legs of his trousers and turned to the coach, oblivious to the small band of people gathering or the dog sniffing at the wheels of the stage.

Ryan straightened. He had more to do than stand around and ogle the newcomer. But when the man at the stage held out his hand to someone inside, and pale, feminine fingers tucked into his, Ryan's curiosity got the best of him. A slender woman in a dress of Montana sky blue descended from the stage, and her crop of red curls fluttered in the light breeze. He thought he caught the scent of flowers but crushed the absurd idea when he considered the distance separating him from the stage. The young woman's expression showed relief as she spoke to the man at her side. Her husband, no doubt. If for no other reason, he had to respect that the man had hitched up with a woman of such beauty.

Ryan turned from the spectacle of the arrivals just as the stocky woman who had passed him minutes before embraced the willowy figure of the younger woman. A long-ago dream burst to the forefront of his desires. He'd wanted a wife once, before his choices had made marrying dangerous. His gaze landed on the young woman again, still caught in the embrace of the elder woman. Her eyes were closed, and a smile brought radiance to her face. When she opened her eyes, she stared straight at Ryan from over the woman's shoulder. She offered a friendly, open smile that neither committed nor encouraged—exactly what he would expect of a married woman. Yet the smile was a punch in the gut, a reminder of what he could have had.

Olivia heard the murmur of Phoebe's voice, even the upward hitch at the end of the string of words that indicated a question, but she couldn't concentrate. The man's eyes bore into hers. He seemed angry, though she didn't understand why. He was a stranger to her. Not a surprise, considering she'd been away from Buffalo for going on ten years. When the man spun on his heel, she traced his path along Main Street with her eyes.

She felt a touch on her elbow, and she pulled back from Phoebe's embrace to see a look of concern on her worn but pleasant face. "I asked if you were feeling well."

"Oh." She patted her hair—a mass of ringlets her aunt's maid had insisted on before she left Kansas. "I'm fine. Just tired."

"No doubt, dear. It's hard to sleep on those rocking conveyances of misery." Phoebe patted her arm. "You stop by Landry's, and we'll serve you up something warm before you make the trek out to your pa's ranch."

Olivia hesitated. She'd been so excited to see her father, yet he was nowhere in sight. "Won't it be too much to feed another mouth at this time of day?"

"Between getting the cattle in, branded, and ready for the drive"—Phoebe shook her head, her reddish-brown hair sweeping her shoulders—"the hands don't come in much during the day in the spring."

Even in her letters, Phoebe Wagner was a chatty woman. Olivia remembered very little of her as a nine-year-old, before her father had sent her east to boarding school, but she'd always looked forward to Phoebe's letters. If only she could say the same about letters from her father. After the first four, he'd never written again, and Phoebe became her only tie to the place she called home.

"Gather that pigheaded pa of yours and get him to bring you to supper sometime if you don't want to stay now. I know you must be excited to see the ranch." Phoebe patted Olivia's cheek, her hand warm and rough. "I'd love to continue this visit, but I have to run. Landry's not often nice enough to let me walk out on a whim, whether or not business is slow. Good thing the stage arrives after lunch." She touched

Olivia's hair "Who would have thought that pale Irish skin and wild red hair would yield such a beauty? Best wear a hat out in this sun though, or those freckles will get worse. And I'll expect a full report on your companion"—she darted a look at the man traveling with Olivia—"as soon as you're settled." And with that, Phoebe wheeled and marched back up Main.

Olivia felt an uncomfortable flare of heat in her neck and turned her head just enough to make sure Tom Mahone had not heard Phoebe's last remark. Her lungs expanded, and she drew an easy breath when she saw him speaking with an older man, who turned and spat into the dust. Olivia grimaced and averted her face, his low chuckle letting her know he'd seen her look of disgust. She hoped the majority of the town had better manners. The stories she'd heard back east about the West made Olivia wonder if she should have heeded her aunt's admonition. *"Westerners are a rough lot"* had become Aunt Fawn's much repeated warning.

Tom Mahone stepped to her side and offered his arm. "I've arranged with the stage driver to load your trunk into a rented wagon. We'll head out to your father's ranch after we eat. Apparently the Occidental is the best place, though Landry's is closer."

Olivia blinked and stared at his arm. "I'd like to head out as soon as possible. It's been ten years, Mr. Mahone. I'm sure you understand my eagerness to be home again."

Tom had picked up the stage in Kansas, and rather than keep her silence, she'd welcomed the easy chatter that had flowed between them. She'd never thought to ask him where he was going, surely not Buffalo. "Don't you need to get back on the stage before it leaves?"

Tom tilted his head and pursed his lips. "I believe Buffalo will suit my purposes just fine. Spinner tells me there's a bigger town close by, and those mountains are something to look at."

Olivia already felt pricks of perspiration. "Spinner?"

"The stage driver." Tom's eyes were sober upon her. "So you won't have supper with me?"

"I'm sure you understand." In the bright sunshine, she saw what the relative darkness of the coach had masked, a two-inch white scar beneath Tom's right eye. It took the edge off his fastidious dress and pale skin. Perhaps the man knew more about life outside an office than she had previously thought.

Without another word, Tom tilted his head to indicate the approaching wagon and helped her up when it rattled to a stop. The driver grunted at her, the same man she'd seen Tom speaking to moments ago. "Good afternoon, ma'am." His grin revealed yellowed teeth. She steeled herself not to react to the disagreeable sight. "I'm Ronald Coltrain."

As the horses pulled the conveyance down the main street, Olivia felt the rise of anticipation. A sudden urge to slip the pins from her hair and twirl in the sunlight captured her fancy, but she only straightened her skirts and folded her hands in her lap.

They passed a barn-shaped house with three dormers on each side of the roof and a sign billing it as the Occidental Hotel. Olivia's eyes took in the quaint building and the out-buildings. As the wagon passed, she glimpsed a man stepping from the hotel. Dark hair, lithe frame, familiar to her… Her heart squeezed in her chest when she caught the man's gaze, and then the wagon rolled past, and she was on her way home.

Chapter 2

Ryan pushed the wide-brimmed hat down on his head to protect himself from the pulsing waves of heat. He had almost decided to take his noon meal in the Occidental's restaurant, but had changed his mind when he found the dining room empty. Landry's restaurant held a handful of patrons. Besides, the rounded woman he'd seen hugging the new arrival might offer up some information on the town. Waitresses tended to glean the latest news from the patrons they served. As he prepared to enter Landry's, the rattle of a wagon made him turn. The curly-headed beauty rode next to Ronald Coltrain. For an instant, their eyes met, until the wagon passed on down the road and he was left with the image of red curls and amber eyes, packaged in a fancy dress of the latest style. Not his type even if she hadn't been married.

He took a table farthest from the door, his back against the wall. The air smelled of the deep flavors of roasted meat but also held a tinge of sweetness. A man with a towel tucked into the waistband of his trousers headed his way, giving off an air of boredom. Probably the type roped into the restaurant business by his wife, who was no doubt tucked back in the kitchen slaving away over steaming pots of the daily special.

"What's smelling good to you tonight, stranger?"

Ryan flicked his gaze over the other people, gauging their reaction to a stranger in their midst. Nobody seemed to show any interest. "Meat. Potatoes. Is that cherry pie I smell?"

"Dried apple."

Ah, he should have known. Cinnamon was the sweet undertone hanging in the air. "I'll have a large slice."

"Name's Robert Landry. If you need anything else, just holler."

"Much obliged." Ryan tilted his head, purposely withholding his name. Landry didn't appear concerned by the omission. He spun on his heel and stopped at a table to inquire after two men. Ryan decided by their dress that they were either ranchers or drifters hoping to get hired for the roundup and drive. And considering they acted as if the food in front of them was their first in days, he guessed they must be drifters.

He considered the handful of others in the restaurant and wondered where the stocky woman was. He had half a mind to saunter toward the kitchen area to see if he could catch a glimpse of her, but he had to be cautious. The problem was not so much in getting information on what had happened to his father, but in trusting those who talked to him to tell the truth. He couldn't hide his identity, not in a small town, but for these first few hours, he wanted to remain nameless and gather as much information as he could on his father's murder.

Landry reappeared with a hot cup of coffee and the pie. He set it down in front of Ryan with a gentleness that belied his size. "You looking for someone, mister?"

"Who's askin'?" he said, careful to measure his movements so he wouldn't appear startled by the question.

"You're not familiar. Thought maybe I could help you along the trail a little faster."

Ryan relaxed in his chair and gave himself time to sip the hot brew before he answered. "Looking for work. Thought there might be some to be had around here."

"You're late into the season. Most have hired out for the

roundups. Could still ride out and see. Some of the bigger spreads might need a hand."

"What's the biggest you got?"

"Rocking S is plenty big, but so's the XR."

Ryan felt tension biting at the nape of his neck. He took a bite of the pie. The cinnamon mixed with the tang of apples was sweet on his tongue. "The Rocking S. That Sattler land?"

Landry turned and started back to the kitchen, not seeming the least affected by his question. A good thing, Ryan reasoned.

"Yup. That's the one," Landry said.

Ryan allowed himself a small smile, congratulating himself on his first victory. He could try to ask more of the man but doubted Landry would be willing or able to sit still long enough. "Is there a woman that works here?" he called out.

"Phoebe?" Landry stopped and turned, brow raised to punctuate the question.

"Red-brown hair?"

"That's her. She had to take plates of food over to the jail. I'll tell her you asked after her."

Ryan took the last bite and sipped his coffee. "No need." He would seek her out later.

Olivia's pulse jumped as they rounded the low hill shielding the entrance to the Rocking S. Despite the clear blue skies, a warm wind traced fingers down her bare neck and sent the curls tickling against her ears. She swiped an errant strand from her eyes and blinked. Her father would know, as Phoebe had, that she was arriving. Her happiness flickered. Of course he wouldn't be standing by the gate, nor the stage, waiting for her. He was a busy man, and she had chosen one of the most hectic times of the year to come home.

"Your father must be beside himself with excitement." Tom's voice was low, his smile beguiling.

"It's been a long time. Everything has changed."

"He will be amazed at the woman you've become."

Olivia refused to look his direction. His kind words bordered on flirtatious, and what had begun innocently enough as two people stuck in the same stagecoach now seemed to hold a trace of something else entirely.

Tom leaned forward and touched her hand. "Would you allow me to come calling? Perhaps we could take supper in town together. Soon." He emphasized the last word.

Olivia's lips parted, but her tongue felt paralyzed. "Perhaps," she finally said. She turned her attention to the corral. The outbuildings looked in fine repair. The curious eyes of men, both on foot and horseback, stared her way.

The wagon stopped rolling, and Olivia rose to her feet almost as soon as the wheels stilled. Without waiting for Tom, she gathered her skirts as close as she dared and hopped to the ground. She heard Tom clear his throat. The driver chortled. "Beat us to it, she did."

She didn't wait to hear more and rushed to the main house, knowing full well she had the attention of every male on the ranch. Her automatic response was to knock, but she laughed and shoved the door inward. "Daddy? Daddy, I'm home!"

An old cowhand raised watery hazel eyes from the wide-plank dining table where he sat. A dusty younger man sat across the table. "There something I can help you with, miss?"

Years fell away as the voice washed over Olivia. "Roper?"

The wiry old Rocking S hand squinted at her and rasped his hand against a covering of mostly gray whiskers. "Livy?"

"Li'l Livy, I believe you called me."

In slow motion, Roper unfolded from the chair, face bright with recognition. "Why, circle the wagons and call me an Indian. You're all grown up!"

"Where's my father?"

The younger man scratched his chair back and rolled to his feet. "Best get back to work, Roper." The man's gingham-blue eyes latched on to her, cold as the lake ice she skated on back east.

"You don't know who this is. This here's Olivia Sattler," Roper offered. "Boss's daughter."

Cold blue eyes snapped to her face then skimmed the length of her. Her skin crawled. "I'm Skinny Bonnet."

"I wanted to see my father." Her flat words were meant to send a warning.

Skinny fingered the edges of his vest. "I'll get him for you. Went down south of the property."

Without another word, he left. Roper remained where he was. "He's the foreman. Has a way of nettling people."

"You speak from experience?"

Roper shrugged. "Not everyone likes him. I'd better git before he starts in on me."

Within seconds Roper was back, her trunk across his back. Heat flared in her cheeks when she recalled its weight and saw the frailty of the man who labored to carry it. "In your room, miss?"

"Yes, please, and thank you so much."

"No problem."

A weight settled on Olivia's shoulders as Roper left and the quietness of the empty house surrounded her. The sharpness of her mother's death penetrated deeper than it had in the years since she'd left. No wonder her father and aunt had decided it best for her to leave Wyoming. She stood at the kitchen table, the same one she remembered from her childhood, and traced the grain of the boards, worn by time and the presence of many hands on its surface. Though neat, the kitchen seemed hollow. Lifeless. And Olivia felt the pang of loneliness so familiar to her at boarding school. Even in the midst of her circle of friends, she'd felt alone when the girls talked of their families and friends, bragging about their privileges and current gossip.

Olivia touched the seat where her mother had presided over the table and felt the coldness of the wood. Sorrow reached down deep into that part of her heart that acknowledged her mother's absence and yanked hard. She would make sure to find her mother's grave, near a shining pond and a tree with arching limbs. It was all she remembered.

With effort she turned her thoughts to taking charge of tasks her mother would have done. Cooking seemed the most obvious. Crossing to the pantry, she assessed the staples along the shelves. Bread would be the perfect beginning, so she lifted down a half-empty sack of flour. Upon straightening, she noticed her mother's apron hanging from a nail beside the shelves. For as long as she could remember, it had been the place Lillian Sattler hung her apron every night after supper. Olivia let the flour sack slide from her grasp and reached a trembling hand to the hard evidence of a presence long gone.

Her eyes closed as she held the delicate white apron against her cheek. Its various smears and smudges and the smell of home and family rolled Olivia back ten years to those times she stood on a stool and watched her mother knead bread or make pies. Even those times her mother shared her favorite peppermints. A rare treat indeed! She tried to bring her mother's face into tighter focus. A face much like her own. She could see her mother's smile as she laughed at one of Olivia's young inanities and smell the fresh peppermint that clung to her when Lily Sattler knelt to hug her close.

Enmeshed in her thoughts, Olivia didn't hear the creak of the front door or the soft steps that drew nearer. A hand clamped her shoulder as her name was spoken. She jerked and turned, hand at her throat. Her father's face greeted her, and she sank into his outstretched arms. Tears burned her eyes and demanded release.

"Welcome home, daughter."

She had no words. Between the surprise of his approach and the reality of his presence after so many years, she could think of nothing to say.

He held her away from him, his smile wide but stiff. As if he'd had little reason to smile for a long time. Craggy wrinkles appeared around his eyes and mouth. His face seemed leaner, darker, more leathery than she remembered. His hair was grayer and thinner.

"You stole my breath," he said. "I thought I was watching your mother."

"Oh Daddy!" She nestled close to him again, releasing the tears that filled her eyes and blurred his image. With her mother's apron in her hands, it was almost like the three of them together again.

"Imagine my surprise to find a beautiful young woman in place of the little girl I sent off so long ago."

"You could have visited. Or sent for me. Or…" Olivia bit her lip and her father pulled back, his hands holding her shoulders.

"And I'm sorry for that. Phoebe told me to visit. I meant to… . It just never seemed the right time to leave.

For ten years? She turned from him, hiding the sheen of tears burning for release. "I'm going to make bread and a cake. Butter cake, your favorite."

His gaze fell to the apron in her hands. "Just like your mother."

She heard the wobble in his voice and turned in time to see his hand wipe at his cheek. She went to him and hugged him hard. He propped his chin on the top of her head. He must feel as she did. Like her mother's ghost had somehow entered the kitchen and orchestrated the tugs of grief from those she loved.

At last her father released her. "I won't have you cooking tonight. Marty will do those honors, butter cake and all. We'll eat that cake up, and you can retire for the evening. Stages aren't big on comfort, and you must be exhausted."

He crossed to the front door, flashed a grin that didn't quite reach his eyes, and was gone. Probably off to raise the alarm to his men that a lady would be present at chuck. Funny how she'd forgotten that her father was not a man of many words. Where she had expected a flowing conversation of news as they played catch-up, she'd received much less.

Her aunt Fawn had tried to warn her about being the only

woman among men. With a sigh, Olivia hooked the apron back on the nail and realized the room had grown dim. Outside the large window, clouds were rolling in. She raised the chimney on a lantern in the center of the table and lit the wick. A welcome splash of light pushed the shadows back as a draft of cold air swept around her ankles.

Chapter 3

"I'm going into town tomorrow, Ryan." Josephine Laxalt stood a full head shorter than her son, but Ryan knew what a determined woman looked like when he saw the tilt of his mother's chin and the gleam in her eyes. "You won't change my mind."

"Father would want me to care for you."

"I, who have cared for others all my life"—Josephine's finger wagged—"need no one to care for me. I will work in town."

Ryan hunkered down in his space at the table and wished he hadn't eaten in town so he could do his mother's greens and ham the honor it deserved. He knew she measured how much he ate—had done so ever since he was a boy. Something about making sure he grew straight and strong. He smiled at the memory of her frowning when he'd reach for a sweet before his plate was clear of the last crumb.

"There are things I can do on the ranch to help you," she said, "but it was Martin's dream, not mine. I want to be with people again, son. You take the ranch. Fulfill your father's dream."

He debated telling his mother that he had reached his decision and would take his father's place—his rightful place—as owner of the Rocking L. Perhaps she wouldn't feel the need to ply him with sumptuous feasts or cry out her grief on his shoulder night after night. He knew her grief was partly due to the fear that she would lose him again to the life he had built away from her.

"You must find a nice young woman. Having warmth in your life will settle you. Make you happier."

He squirmed in his seat, feeling very much like a quivering lizard in the hand of a small boy. Twenty-six years old and still a child in his mother's eyes. Yet no anger burned through him at the thought. His mother had worked hard all her life. She was generous and kind, loving and stern. But there was something else at stake, and Ryan struggled to understand his mother's blindness to the obvious.

"He was killed, Mama."

Her hands stilled then knotted together and rested on the edge of the table. She stared at her plate.

"You know it's true," he said. "It's what brought me home and what I must do to—"

"It is not your fight." His mother's voice was a harsh whisper—as fierce as he'd ever heard it. "Your father believed things could be made right peaceably."

"And that attitude got him killed."

His mother's head came up. Her dark eyes were placid yet determined. "Because you do not understand, just as your father did not understand."

He pressed his lips together. "What is it I don't understand?"

"That these men do not want peace. They want war."

"Then I'll give them war."

"By doing so, you would leave me alone. You think you can hold back the force that is against us, but it is too great. There are too many of them." Her hand chopped the air. "It is not your fight."

"If I'm to be a rancher, I must try."

She gasped. "You will run the ranch then?"

"Yes. I'll have Bobby hire more men to help ready for the drive."

"They will fight you even in the roundup. Claiming unbranded cattle as their right, no matter whose property the animal is on."

He absorbed her words. "I won't let them."

"You will become their enemy."

"Father's way did not work. Let me try my own methods."

His mother bowed her head. "Yours will not work either."

"I'll use caution."

Her slim shoulders rose and fell on a sigh. "I will cook for you and keep the house, but I will work in town, too."

His mother stood to her feet and gathered her plate. Black hair curled in tendrils around her face, softening the lines bracketing her eyes.

"Who did it, Mama? Tell me."

Her spine stiffened. Without replying, she plunged the dirty dish into a bucket and swirled it around. "I will not speculate. It is dangerous. What is done is done." A lone tear slipped down her cheek. She smeared it away with a wet hand. "Your father is gone and cannot return to us."

If Olivia thought home meant pleasant days spent in lengthy conversation with her devoted father, she'd been out in the Wyoming sun too long. Jay Sattler never sat longer than necessary to eat before he rose, kissed her cheek, and was out the door.

It had been three days since Olivia's arrival on the stage. In those days she had cleaned every corner of the ranch house and cooked all the meals except that first one. Any attempts to open a real conversation usually fell flat after a few monosyllabic answers from her father. She wanted more than anything to sit down and cry, and she knew just the person whose shoulder she wanted to saturate.

In her room she contemplated her gowns—fussy styles and materials that would never hold up out here. She wanted something that gave her the freedom to ride. Thinking of her mother's clothes, she wandered into the room her parents used to share. The pegs on the wall held nothing more than a pair of her father's trousers. She chided herself. It made sense that her father would have packed or given away her mother's clothes.

Olivia crossed to her own room and debated over the gowns again. She had one brown day dress that had very little adornment, though the style was in keeping with the use of a bustle. Olivia had made the decision to leave all her bustles with her aunt, trying to travel as lightly as possible. Aunt Fawn had put up a fuss, lecturing her about "proper dress" and "stylish women of fine education," but Olivia had been adamant, mollifying her aunt by suggesting she could order one once she arrived in Buffalo. Her aunt's glower had given voice to her doubts, but Olivia had remained firm, and the bustles had stayed in Aunt Fawn's care.

Olivia hugged herself, delighted to be free of the constraints of fashion. Huge bustles, restrictive corsets…

Aunt Fawn would swoon.

She yanked the lid off a hatbox and pulled out her top hat. A must for any riding costume back east. With a grin of delight, Olivia stuffed the hat back into the box. She'd be trading a top hat for a wide-brimmed western one as soon as she could. Her day seemed to take on a life of its own. She changed into the brown gown, frowning at the added length going bustleless added in the back and sides, but fingering the silky material and appreciating the expense that had gone into it. Funny how she'd never considered her mother's simple styles compared to Aunt Fawn's lust for the latest fashion, not to mention her insistence that Olivia dress accordingly.

Now she would be free of all that, and it felt good. Right, somehow. Though Aunt Fawn had made her feel welcome, there was always an underlying coldness. Or maybe oblivion was a better word. Aunt Fawn didn't know there was a world beyond her own, making her incapable of understanding Olivia's confusion when she compared her mother to Jay Sattler's older sister. Fawn's stiff smile never failed to show her displeasure when the subject of her brother's ranch operation came up, and Olivia realized she'd always resented that silent disapproval.

No matter. She was here now, and despite what her father thought she should do to occupy her time, Olivia had no intention of spending her days twiddling her fingers. She could keep the housework up without problem, but she intended to find a job. In Buffalo. As soon as possible.

Chapter 4

"You could work at the saloon as a barmaid."

Olivia gasped at her friend's straight-faced suggestion. "Phoebe Wagner!"

"You'd get a fistful of tips."

Before Olivia could sputter her utter disbelief, she saw the mischievous spark in her friend's dark eyes. "How terrible of you."

Phoebe spat a laugh as she set a cup of coffee in front of her friend and took the seat opposite. "Thought that might take the starch out of you."

"Am I that bad?"

"When you got off that stagecoach, I thought the queen had come west."

Olivia studied the rim of her cup and the chip in the handle. The words settled over her more like an observation than a rebuke. "It's a change."

"Got that right. But you're here now, and you'll adjust. Your mama was a kindhearted woman, and underneath all that starch your aunt rubbed on ya, you'll be one of us in no time."

"Tell me about her."

Phoebe tugged at a wild bright red curl and shrugged. "What's to tell? She was a good woman. She gave me a chance when I needed it and taught me what my drunken pa never could."

Olivia sipped the bitter, hot brew, made a face that drew a laugh from Phoebe, and plunked her cup back down. "When did Daddy let you go?"

"After you left."

Olivia studied her friend's small apartment over the rim of the coffee cup. There wasn't much to look at. Phoebe lived simply. Olivia had never known ostentation until she'd lived with Aunt Fawn, and then she'd accepted it as a new normal. Her father's home reflected the same simplicity as Phoebe's. Self-conscious now, Olivia frowned at her gown.

Phoebe laughed. "We'll get you over to the dressmaker. She can make you some sensible clothing. No use wearing those draperies in this heat."

"It's the latest style."

"Latest style or not, it's best put away for visits to Aunt Fawn." Phoebe drained the last of her coffee. "I need to get myself back downstairs or Landry will have my hide."

"Is he hiring?"

"Sure he is." Phoebe glanced over her shoulder. "But your schooling is best put to use doing something else. You said you enjoyed writing. Why not ask Jon at the paper if you can work as a journalist?"

"A journalist?"

"Why not? Didn't you work for that fancy Philly paper for a time?"

"I wrote a couple of articles that the *Inquirer* bought." She lowered her voice. "Mostly on fashion, but only because Aunt Fawn drilled me on the latest trends. It was dreadfully boring."

"Really now?" Phoebe's smile was bright. Too bright. "I promise you won't miss the bustles, bows, stays, and braces once you've done without them."

Fancy frippery and fine footwear were all the things embraced back in Philly. She tilted her head and thought on it a bit. "But I look forward to fitting in and being a western girl again."

"You always were a bit of a tomboy."

"Yes, I suppose I was. Maybe that's why Aunt Fawn was so determined to dress me to her liking."

"And now"—Phoebe opened the door—"I've got to get downstairs. Let me know what you find over at the paper."

Left to herself, Olivia found the small, one-story building with Buffalo Bulletin written on a board and mounted above the door. The smell of ink and oil made her nose twitch. A lone man was bent over a tray, shuffling through tiny, ink-stained blocks. He didn't acknowledge her presence, and despite three desks tucked into a corner of the room hinting at other employees, no one else came forward.

"Good morning, sir."

She frowned when he didn't respond. For all intents and purposes, the man didn't look old. He certainly wasn't old enough to have hearing problems.

"Good morning?" She tried again.

The man's hands paused. He squinted at the tray, wiped his forehead with the back of his hand, and continued his search for another letter. Olivia cleared her throat for a third try, determined to make sure her voice projected this time, when the door opened behind her.

"Miss Sattler. What a pleasure."

The wheat-brown hair, longer on the collar, and his trim mustache and pale skin were a welcome sight. "Mr. Mahone."

Tom Mahone took her hand in his and squeezed, delight making dimples in his cheeks. Olivia didn't miss the light of admiration in his eyes. "How is Marv treating you?"

She followed Tom Mahone's gaze to the back of the man sifting through the small blocks of wood. His voice dropped. "Marv is shy. Especially around women. He's a good worker though."

Worker?

Tom stepped back and spread his arms. "The paper is mine now."

Marv turned from his work to glance wide-eyed at his employer. His eyes grazed across Olivia. His hand hit a container, and letters spilled to the floor. Olivia watched as the man stooped to pick up the pieces. When she moved to help, Tom touched her elbow.

"Marv can clean it up. I'm much more interested in hearing about the reason for this delightful visit. Perhaps it is too much to hope that you were coming to see me?"

"I don't know how I could be when I didn't know you owned the paper." Indeed, even Phoebe, the woman whose finger was on the pulse of Buffalo, had still thought the paper was owned by another.

"Jon was ready for retirement." Tom turned, unable to see the moment when Marv again raised his head, stabbing his employer with his eyes. When he caught Olivia watching him, he returned to his scramble for the pieces.

"I need a reporter. Didn't you tell me on the way over that you did some work for the *Philadelphia Inquirer*?"

Olivia flinched. "Why, yes…"

"There now. A woman like you must be bored sitting on a ranch all day. Take up a pencil, and let's get to reporting. I've already picked up the latest on the flood that occurred in Johnstown."

In the coach, Tom had seemed like such a laid-back gentleman, but his manner now seemed brusque, cocky. Olivia frowned, trying to sort her feelings and still follow the conversation. Something about Johnstown. "Pennsylvania?"

Tom dragged a chair from behind the desk and offered it to her. "Please."

She gathered the yards of her skirt in one hand and slipped into the chair, suddenly aware of her ill-fitting gown. "You were saying about Johnstown?"

"Flooded. Looking at almost ten thousand dead."

She had heard of the town, especially the elaborate hunting and fishing club, whose membership was a source of great envy for her aunt Fawn. But what Tom was saying didn't make sense.

"The dam burst and sent a geyser of water down the hillside. Terrible, simply terrible." He perched on the edge of the desk and waved a hand in dismissal. "What I really want to know is if you'll take the job."

She held up her hand. "Tom, slow down."

He braced his knuckles against his knee and leaned forward. Devilment emanated from his eyes and the twist of his mouth. Even the scar on his cheek seemed to pucker into a half-moon grin. "I'll pay you exactly what I would pay a man—an offer you won't find in most men-only small towns. How can you refuse?"

Chapter 5

Streams of morning light played off Josephine Laxalt's hair. Every angle of her body and face spoke of her stubborn determination to get a job in town. They'd spent breakfast discussing—no, *arguing* would be the better word—over the wisdom and necessity of such a move. Ryan didn't want to think about it anymore. His mother's mind was made up, and his ability to sway her was nonexistent. The only man who could change his mother's mind was dead, and he was even beginning to question his father's success rate.

His mother swayed on the wagon seat, her right hand clenched along the edge to secure her position. He groaned in frustration. Women! Or maybe that should be *mothers*!

When did she get to be so stubborn? He relaxed his hands on the reins. He'd always wondered where his own stubbornness came from. The thought helped to snuff his irritation. "Where do you want to go exactly?"

They rode along for a minute in utter silence. When Ryan stole a sideways glance at his mother, he witnessed the softening. She now stared at her lap then lifted her dark eyes to his.

"Phoebe might help me find a job. Stop right there in front of the sign that says Landry's."

He didn't bother to tell her he knew the place. When he

brought the wagon to a halt, he set the brake and hurried to the other side of the wagon, half-expecting his mother to vault to the ground. She did't. Instead, she beamed a beautiful, charming smile at him. And because of that warm charisma, he could see why his father had run into trouble being angry at his mother.

"You're a charmer."

She placed her hand along his cheek, her grin fading. "And you, my son, are as well. Flash that beautiful smile at some young woman, and she will be yours forever. You've a good heart." Tears puddled in her eyes. She turned away and dabbed at her eyes.

Ryan brushed his fingers through his hair. He felt weighted with weariness. A cowboy rode by, his horse's hooves kicking up a cloud of dust. He moved to his horse's head and scratched along the animal's cheek, debating his next step and the wrath of his mother's disapproval if he stirred the debate over her working in town.

Across the street, the door to the *Buffalo Bulletin* yanked open. Through the dissipating dust, he could see heavy brown fabric and recognized the auburn beauty he'd seen at the stage office days ago. She moved as if in a trance. Ryan flinched as she began to step into the street. A team of oxen pulling a wagon barreled down the center of Main. The driver stood and yelled. The woman didn't appear to hear. When she stepped out into the path of the wagon, Ryan sprinted across the street. His boots plowed dust as his right arm hooked her waist. Her eyes widened, and a little scream wrenched from her lips. He drove her backward, lifting her off her feet. Trace chains rattled, and the curses of the driver rained down on them as the wagon bolted past.

Ryan spread his left hand at her back to help her keep her balance as she recovered. She blinked at him, dazed.

"My pardon, ma'am. Those oxen were moving fast."

"No. I—"

Up close he could see the spray of freckles across her nose.

It gave her the look of an imp, albeit a beautiful one. Her light auburn hair tickled the slender column of her neck. Ryan swallowed and straightened, and when their eyes met, the jump in his pulse forced him to draw air into his suddenly starved lungs.

"I'm afraid…" She gave a little laugh and glanced down. He realized his arm still curved around her waist. Her husband would take offense if she didn't.

Ryan jerked his hand back as a crushing wave of retribution washed over him. He turned away. "Be careful crossing the street."

A lilt of laughter caught him midstride, and the silken brush of her hand at his elbow coaxed him to turn and face her. "I will be more careful, kind sir. And thank you. I fear my mind was far away. Do you…? Might I know your name?"

Too late Ryan remembered to remove his hat. She must think him a dolt. He certainly felt like one. "Laxalt. Ryan Laxalt."

"Thank you, Mr. Laxalt. As my first article for the *Buffalo Bulletin*, I shall write on the danger of not watching where one is going while crossing a busy street."

He caught the twinkle of mirth in her gaze, but a withering self-rebuke tightened his stomach. "Leave my name out of it unless you want blood on your hands." A look of dismay slashed her features, and he turned on his heel and stalked off. Anger welled at his harsh tone. All she had done was tease, but the gentle jab of fun had hit him square. To have his presence announced in such a public manner would surely bring the wrath of his father's murderer down on his head before he could do his own investigation.

Olivia watched Ryan leave, her spirit stale after his harsh words. His dress pegged him as a cowboy. She didn't intend on wasting another second thinking of his gray eyes and dark hair. That he'd saved her was one thing, but his hard dismissal was, well, rude. Beyond rude. Reprehensible. Aunt Fawn would sniff and tsk-tsk and encourage her to move along.

But Olivia watched him go against her will. His ground-eating stride exposed his eagerness to be away from her as much as the level of his anger. *Blood on her hands?* She'd done nothing wrong. *And, no, Mr. Laxalt, I won't write an article about you, unless it is to eschew rude manners and name you as an example.* That would require the use of his name though.

With a sigh, she picked up her skirts and gave a yank to the heavy material. Nothing to clear a mind like the idea of a new dress. She glanced up and down Main and was relieved to see a store two doors down from where she stood. She would begin there.

Even as she stepped toward the store, she felt compelled to glance over her shoulder. No sign of Ryan Laxalt. The slightest tug of disappointment nagged. Her foot caught in the folds of material, and she tripped. She grabbed at a post that sliced a splinter into her palm. Tears collected at the burn of the injury. It had wedged deep into her skin. And it was long. She rubbed the area around the splinter with her free hand and kicked at the excess material pooled around her feet. Feeling much like a horse pulling a wagon, she let the unwieldy material drag through the dust on the road. She was determined to be done with all her fancy gowns once and for all.

Pushing inside the store, she paused to inhale the familiar scents of wood, leather, and spices. It was a smell like no other—and one that settled her, cloaking her in familiarity. A short, balding man set aside the paper hiding his face and greeted her with a smile.

"I heard you'd come home to Wyoming, little Livy Sattler." His friendly face creased into wrinkles that hadn't been quite so deep ten years ago. Still, Olivia would never forget Papa Don.

Looking into that kind face stripped away the years, and she was suddenly the small child at her mother's side ordering a stick of candy in a shy voice and hiding her face in her mother's skirts. A knot formed in her throat.

Papa Don stopped at his candy display and, eyes twinkling, plunged his hand into the peppermint jar. He held out the sweet to her as he closed the distance between them. Tears threatened when she closed her hand around the candy. Papa's face blurred beneath the onslaught of her tears, and she felt him press a kerchief into her hand.

"It's the memories, isn't it, child?" His soothing voice rolled over her as she sniffed. Aunt Fawn would have been mortified at her public display, but she didn't care. This wasn't Philadelphia. "When I lost my dear Ellen five years back, it was so hard to come back to the store."

She sniffed and did her best to push back the emotion. "I'm so sorry. I don't know what came over me. I just… The smell seemed so familiar and—"

"No need to explain. I guess a woman has a right to some tears."

How could she have forgotten Papa Don's kindness? He'd always had the utmost patience while she looked over the candy selection. His wife had been a rosy-cheeked woman with a quick laugh and pleasant voice, good for a pat on the head or compliment. In that little-girl place of her heart, she'd wished they were her grandmother and grandfather, because her real ones were so very far away.

"Mama Ellen…" She paused to consider how easily the familiar title slipped from her tongue.

"Took sick and never could shake it."

She held out her hands to the older man, and he took them. "I have such fond memories of her."

"She always had a soft spot for you, Miss Livy. Now"—he squeezed her hands and let go then extended his arms out to take in the goods surrounding them—"what can Papa Don do for you?"

"I need some dresses made. Is there anyone in town who could make them, or could I order some?"

A draft of hot air rushed and swirled around them, announcing someone's entrance. Papa Don lifted his head and waved. "I'll be with you in a moment, Mrs. Laxalt."

Olivia caught the image of a dark-haired woman who was shorter than her by a foot. She saw the woman's nod and heard her soft, accented "Thank you, Papa Don." Olivia wasn't sure what it was about the woman's voice that drew her, but she watched as the woman made her way to a corner of the store that held fabric, thread, and other sundries.

When she turned back to Papa Don, the sun seemed to rise in his smile. He, too, followed the departing back of his patron. He jerked his head in Mrs. Laxalt's direction and said, "That's the woman for you. Sews a streak from what I hear." His voice dropped even lower. "Probably could use some extra money right now, being she just lost her husband. Came in earlier asking if I'd advertise for her in the window. I told her she could make use of the new sewing machine I got in." He winked. "Best advertisement for merchandise I could hope for."

A new widow. Olivia's heart ached for the woman. To have loved and lost… And she didn't appear to be that old. Early fifties.

"If you want, I can ask her," Papa Don offered.

"Timing is everything, and God's timing is perfect," her mother's voice whispered through her head. It had been part of a Bible lesson long forgotten, but stirred now because it fit the circumstances. Olivia shook her head. "It'll give me a chance to introduce myself."

Without waiting to hear whatever response was forming on Papa Don's lips, Olivia crossed to the dark-haired woman rubbing at the splinter tip.

"Would you happen to have a needle to get a splinter out?" The woman's smile pinched to concern, and her gentle touch and soothing words as she worked to dislodge the splinter was the balm Olivia's heart needed.

Upon closer inspection, she could see better the simplicity of the woman's dress and the strands that had escaped the brush. More white than black threaded through her shiny hair, albeit more heavily on the right temple than on the left. Her eyes flashed with bright alertness yet held a softness that promised long hugs and tables heavy with the favorite dishes of her loved ones. Beautiful eyes. Soulful and loving.

Chapter 6

Ryan knew a man's chances of picking up local information revolved around the saloon, the livery, and the store. He began at the livery, hoping he would not have to enter the saloon at all, out of respect for his mother's reputation among the townsfolk. But should the need arise, he would have little choice. His worries found relief when he saw a boy working a shoe onto a horse.

"Your pa around?"

"No, sir."

"He own this place?"

"Yes, sir." The boy let go of the horse's leg and straightened, wiping a thin line of sweat from his brow. "He leaves me in charge most days. You needin' a horse?"

"No. Not today anyhow. I was just wondering if you knew anything about the shooting that took place here a couple weeks ago."

The boy's light gray eyes grew wary. "You the law?"

Ryan spit a laugh he didn't feel. "Just curious to know what people are saying about who did it. Name's Ryan."

"Lance Daniels." The boy set aside his mallet and stuck out his hand. He gave Ryan's arm quite the workout. Whatever the boy was, he wasn't weak. His slim build covered lean muscle. "Most 'round here think Laxalt got what was coming to him. Stealing cattle's a hanging offense."

Hot denial came to his tongue. Ryan clenched his jaw. Best to let the boy talk.

"Skinny found Sattler cattle in with Laxalt's." The boy shrugged. "Seems clear that Laxalt was jealous of the big ranchers and decided they could spare a few head to fatten his herd."

"Who's Skinny?"

"Sattler's foreman."

"That's a strong accusation."

"Sattler, Bowman, and Michaels are pretty much the law 'round here."

"Nobody thought to investigate the accusation?"

Lance leaned against a stall door and shrugged. "Why would he lie?"

Ryan touched the brim of his hat. "Good question." He pivoted, and a trace of dust rose around his feet. "I'll be sure to use your services when I'm in town. Horse could use some new shoes."

"Bring him over, mister. We'll take care of him."

His business concluded, Ryan crossed to Landry's. The woman who seated him was the same one he'd seen hugging on the beauty he'd held in his arms earlier. Better not to dwell on the way she had felt against him. He had done what any man would have done in his place, but she was not his to think about.

"Sit anywhere." The woman motioned. "Name's Phoebe."

Ryan scanned the few people in the restaurant and saw no sign of his mother. Phoebe set a lemonade in front of him and hovered at his elbow as he studied the two choices scribbled on a piece of slate at the back of the dining room.

"I'll have the chicken."

She was coarse of face and round, but her smile was bright and her expression open and honest. She looked to Ryan's eye like a woman quite capable of caring for herself. That his mother would be friends with such a woman shouldn't surprise him.

After replaying the boy's heavy accusation and considering the general restlessness he'd read about since arriving, Ryan thought he might understand his mother's concern. If the townsfolk thought his father guilty, proving otherwise would be hard work. The experience he had in such matters would come in handy. And there was no excuse for a man accused of rustling getting a bullet in the back. A man had a right to face his accuser. He didn't plan on resting until he found the person who'd killed his father. His muscles suddenly burned with the need to move, and he wished he hadn't ordered. Phoebe appeared with his food and set it down.

"My mother. She was coming to talk to you."

Phoebe's eyes widened. "Your mother?"

"She was going to ask you about"—he swallowed—"about finding a job in town."

Phoebe remained still, palm flat on the table, brows lowered. "Josephine Laxalt?"

He hesitated. "Yes." He shook off the chagrin. It was time to let it be known he was home.

"Haven't seen her today." Her eyes shifted to the windows at his back, and her smile appeared, triumphant and playful. "But I think I just found her. She's with Olivia right there."

Ryan twisted on his seat to follow the woman's finger then stood to get a better view. His mother stood with her back to him, talking to the woman he'd rescued not even an hour before.

"She's a pretty one, isn't she? You've not met her yet?"

"We've met," he managed to say. When his mother and Olivia turned and headed for Landry's, a blast of nerves assaulted him. He put a hand down to steady himself, and warmth oozed over it, soft and squishy. He closed his eyes in horror over what he'd just done and inhaled as a titter of laughter squeaked from Phoebe.

"Here you go."

He opened his eyes to see the square of cloth Phoebe held out to him. Her face was red and her eyes much too bright. She hicupped on a giggle as he withdrew his hand from the mashed potatoes and accepted the cloth. With quick wipes, he rid his palm and fingers of the mess.

Phoebe greeted the women as they drew closer.

"Ryan, what are you doing here?"

"Finished my business early. I thought you said you'd be here." He didn't even try to keep the accusation from his voice.

His mother stiffened. "I am not the child, son."

"Forgive me, Mama, but there's much to worry about when I know we have enemies."

His mother gave him a tight smile then turned to indicate the woman at her side. "I want you to meet my new employer, Miss Olivia."

Ryan's head whipped upward, and the woman his mother pressed forward gave him an awkward smile. "I believe we've met."

"You crossed the road without looking." He tried to inject humor into his voice.

"Thank you for caring." Her words were mild, but her eyes flashed.

He dragged in a breath. She had whiskey eyes, though he was sure she would hate that description. Her eyelashes swept down over cheeks splashed pink from sun, exertion, or natural color—he didn't know which. Ryan stood to his feet, more aware of her than he wanted to be.

"Let's sit down and eat," his mother said. When he caught her eye, a twinkle sparked in those familiar brown depths. One of those amused looks she shot him every time he'd let loose with a lie as a child. Why, then, was he surprised when his mother sat across from him, leaving Olivia the spot beside him as the only choice. "Ryan, would you help…"

"Why is there a…?" He followed Olivia's eyes as she took the seat he held for her and realized evidence of his sloppiness—soiled napkin and palm print in the potatoes—lay for all to see. And laugh at. "Perhaps you should watch where you place your hand, Mr. Laxalt."

Too late Olivia felt the heat of a blush as she realized how that comment might sound. She pointed at the potatoes to emphasize what she referred to. Ryan Laxalt's eyes shone. Whether with mischief or guarded amusement, she couldn't quite tell, but at least he didn't offer a leering look.

Shoving back the offending plate, he resumed his seat. Despite his earlier terseness, she noted that he was able to admit his wrongs. Well, at least to his mother. His earlier flash of anger stuck in her mind like a burr.

"Miss Olivia asked me to sew some dresses for her," Mrs. Laxalt said. "She needs proper clothes for the West."

"Especially this heat."

Ryan's eyes rolled over her, touching what he could see of the gown. When his eyes raised to hers, a stab of awareness tilted her world off balance. It had to be his eyes. Curious eyes. Pale yet not pale at all. His dark hair curled at the ends but was longer than she'd seen most men wear.

"Papa Don said he would allow me to set up shop in that back corner of the store where he keeps his materials. I can work there and be out of your way, son. Others might even ask me to sew."

"If that is what you wish, Mother."

The hard clench of his jaw contradicted his easy statement. Olivia wondered at his reluctance. Was his displeasure aimed at her working in general? Or maybe at Josephine working for Papa Don or even herself?

"You are God's blessing to me this day, Miss Olivia," Josephine said.

Phoebe chose that moment to materialize with tall glasses of lemonade. "It'll clear the dust from your throat. Hello, Mrs. Laxalt. Your son was just asking after you."

Josephine favored Phoebe with a smile and reached to pat Ryan's hand. "He is a good boy to worry over his mama. I was to come to you and ask for work, but this young woman has asked me to sew for her."

Phoebe's smile seemed to sag.

"All will be well, Phoebe," Josephine soothed.

Not understanding Josephine's words to Phoebe—almost a reassurance of sorts—Olivia looked to Ryan. His silver eyes flashed, and his dark brows lowered like clouds heavy with storm.

Josephine seemed eager to smooth the moment, and before Olivia could form a question that might clear the fog, she smiled. "I'll be in town tomorrow to begin. Will you be able to come in and be measured?"

"I have work to do on the ranch." Ryan formed the words on stiff lips.

Josephine's hand reached to pat his shoulder. "I can get into town by myself. No use you thinking you have to escort me in and out."

"Doesn't the Laxalt ranch border ours?" Olivia asked. "I could come by and pick you up in the mornings until we're done settling on materials and…"

Phoebe's panicked eyes flashed to Ryan then Josephine, and beside her, Olivia felt the stiffening of Ryan's posture. The storm in his eyes broke, and his lips formed a thin line.

Josephine reached to squeeze her son's hand where it white-knuckled his glass of lemonade.

"You're a Sattler?" He spit the words.

Olivia flinched and leaned away from him, singed by the heat of his question. "Jay Sattler is my father."

Chapter 7

"You knew, Mama." Ryan tried his best to contain his rage and confusion as he guided the wagon along the road out of town. He stared at the horse's ears because he could not look at his mother. "I'm trying to understand."

"I met her in the store, and she needed clothes. I need work."

"Not this. No. I can take care of you. The ranch will support us as it always supported you and Father."

"It is not your decision, and I don't want you to get involved."

He rolled his head on his shoulders to relieve the rising tension biting into his neck. "Sattler killed Papa. That does involve me."

"You do not know for certain."

He couldn't believe his mother's stubbornness on the issue. It should have been clear to her why he had to wedge himself into the situation. What kind of son would he be if he heard the news of his father's death and didn't return home to care for his mother?

Josephine's lips compressed.

"He was accused of rustling cattle. That's stealing."

"And you think your father would do such a thing?"

"No. Of course not. But that's why I need to clear his name of this accusation. To find out who killed him and why the accusation was made in the first place. Until then, I ask that you not be seen with Olivia Sattler."

"Because she's a Sattler?" His mother's expression grew dark with disapproval.

"And you're a Laxalt."

She drew herself erect. "I would hope by now that you realize the sins of one don't reflect on anyone but the person doing the sin. Olivia Sattler just arrived in town yesterday after years spent in Philadelphia."

"I know that." At least he knew that she'd just arrived in town.

"Then you must understand that her role in anything involving us is only in your head."

He stiffened at that and slapped the reins against the horse's rump.

"Stop punishing the horse," his mother bit out. Her hand clasped the side of the seat as the wagon lurched forward.

Chastened, Ryan pulled gently on the reins. The horse slowed. "If I don't do this, Mama, I would never forgive myself. He was my—"

"Would he want you to ride the trail of revenge?"

"Would he, or is it your wish that I avoid the trail?"

"Then it is revenge you want."

"Justice."

His mother released a heavy breath, and her voice was low and terse. "They will kill you, Ryan. I can't bear to lose you, too."

On impulse he hauled back on the reins and set the hand brake. "You've refused to tell me anything. Tell me now. Convince me there is no need for me to find the truth." He bit the inside of his cheek and his eyes scanned over the blue horizon that framed his mother's small form.

When her dark head dipped and he heard a sniffle, Ryan clamped his eyes shut. Nothing could diminish him to a bumbling, penitent blob of boyhood like seeing his mother cry. Dutifully he yanked the kerchief form his back pocket and pressed it against the back of his mother's hand.

"Mama…"

"If something were to happen to you, my heart would break completely."

He didn't understand. He had been away from home for years. He could have died several times over, and she wouldn't have known for weeks, maybe even months or years. But now, because he was nearby, she suddenly feared him dying? Maybe he did understand her point. He shook his head. No, not really.

"Do you know what it would be like to have not only my husband but my son murdered as well?"

His spine went rigid. His jaw hardened. "So he was murdered."

Her mouth flew open. "Yes. No. Ryan, listen to me. You must not do this thing that you think you need to do. They will hunt you down as they have others—"

"Others?" If her tears had made him indecisive, the idea that Sattler made victims of others steeled his resolve. Without saying a word, he released the brake and set the wagon into motion. Rays of sunshine waned, weakened by impending evening, and a cooling breeze sifted over his neck and face. His mother remained quiet, chin lifted high, but the quiver of her lips told him her tears were just below the surface of her composure.

"I only want peace."

He released a heavy sigh, his words soft. "Sometimes, Mama, you cannot have peace until you have waged a war."

Olivia pressed the hat down on her head and tilted it to observe the effect in the mirror. Saucy, but the look was too overconfident for her. Plus she wasn't in Philadelphia. She doubted very seriously that Wyoming women would have need for a small hat angled to effect. Besides, if the sun was any indicator, those wide-brimmed hats she'd seen on so many since arriving would serve better to keep her fragile skin from breaking out in sun-induced freckles. Tucking the hat back into the box, she heard her father's boots on the front porch. Her heart sank at his arrival. At the discussion she would have to have with him. She placed the hatbox on her bed and smoothed the front of her bustleless gown. Tomorrow morning and the promise of sensible clothes could not come soon enough.

Olivia took one more look at herself in the mirror and frowned. She hoped Ryan Laxalt's dark attitude toward her would not demand his mother break the agreement for those dresses. Josephine's sadness had been palpable after Olivia had spoken her father's name. Ryan had left the table without so much as a "good day." But the worst part had been the conversation with Phoebe that had followed.

As she had watched Josephine meet up with her son outside the restaurant, his face a mask of controlled rage, Olivia had demanded that Phoebe explain why the sound of her father's name had brought such a reaction.

Phoebe had twisted her hands together in abject misery. "It's a long story."

"Without my dinner companions, I have plenty of time for conversation."

Scanning the dining room with a hopeful look, as if a patron might enter at any second and rescue her from the conversation, Phoebe grimaced and sank to the vacated chair. "It's an old problem."

"Old? As in something that has happened since I left?"

The transformation in Phoebe startled Olivia. Her friend's face went pale, and she slumped somewhat. "Your father is not well liked around here, Livy."

Not. Well. Liked. A troubling thought perhaps, but something Olivia felt could be shrugged off—if not for Phoebe's reaction. That alone spelled trouble of the worst kind. "There is no need to shield me from things, Phoebe. I am not a child."

Phoebe had cupped her hands around the lemonade. She flicked off beads of condensation, and the drops scattered and fell to the floor. Phoebe smoothed the dew from another side of the mug and rubbed her hands together, never once meeting Olivia's gaze. She waited, calculating that for Phoebe to show such reluctance to broach the subject, the news must not be good. Somehow Olivia was not surprised. Hadn't her father been distant? As if circumstances tied him in knots. Nothing like the jovial, lighthearted man she remembered. Or was that the ideology of a young child biased toward her daddy?

"There's a silent war taking place."

Olivia remained still as Phoebe hesitated. "The big ranchers seem intent on creating problems for the small ranchers. I think the attitude is that all land belongs to the big ranches, and that the little ranchers and farmers should yield their land, their cattle—everything. A small rancher south of here was found murdered about three months ago. Sheriff said he had news the man was a rustler."

"They murder rustlers?"

"Normally hang them."

Olivia shuddered. "How terrible." But what does it have to do with my father and the Laxalts?"

"Couple weeks ago there was a shooting. Martin Laxalt was found dead, shot through the heart."

Another murder? Olivia felt the blood drain from her face. Ryan Laxalt was thinking her father was responsible for the shooting that had killed his father? "Ryan's father rustled cattle?"

Phoebe shrugged. "Depends on who you ask."

Something squeezed her throat and shallowed her breathing. Phoebe jumped to her feet, but Olivia sucked in a great breath of air and motioned her friend down. "It's impossible. Tell me it's impossible. My father could never do such a terrible deed."

Phoebe reached out and squeezed her hand. "We're not

saying your father pulled the trigger, but he might have had a hand in…"

Disbelief raged through Olivia. That her father could be so accused was unthinkable. "I thought you were our friend."

"I am your friend, Livy. But your father has changed over the years."

Weighted by the insinuation, Olivia bolted from her seat, unable to hear more. Phoebe hadn't tried to stop her.

The trip home had been long, but Olivia had used it to do some serious thinking. There was only one way to clear her father's name, and her new job at the paper might be useful in allowing her to dig around and ask questions without raising suspicion. Her father had to be innocent, because the opposite was too unbearable to consider.

Chapter 8

Ryan waited out front of the store. His mother wasn't happy with him, and he knew it. Not only had he turned a deaf ear to her talk of getting herself into town, but when she'd laid eyes on the rifle he clamped beneath his arm, Ryan had realized his error.

"You cannot do this." She grasped his forearm.

Josephine Laxalt's eyes held horror and pain, and Ryan felt remorse in every sinew and muscle. She didn't understand, and no matter how hard he tried, she never would. But he should have thought better of hauling along the rifle and inadvertently showing his intentions. He did the only thing he could do. He equivocated. "I'm riding the fence after dropping you in town. I might need the protection. And if anyone troubles us…"

He knew by the sidelong glance his mother gave that she saw right through his words.

"Whoever killed Father might just think it best to finish off you and me. It's our land they want, Mama, and we stand in their way." He placed his hand on her shoulder. "Please, let me handle this."

They rode to town in silence as the sun stretched higher in the sky and the cool breeze of night yielded to waves of familiar heat. Few people stirred in town this early, and those who did either affected oblivion at his presence or raised a hand in greeting. He wondered if the silent message his presence at the Lazy L sent was even now being stewed over by those who thought his father their enemy. Ryan hoped so.

"Wait for me," his mother said as they pulled up to the store. "I will make sure Papa Don is ready for me before you leave."

Minutes stretched, and Ryan grew restless, even fearful for his mother. He'd just lifted his foot to beat a path to the door when his mother popped out, Olivia Sattler at her heels. The red-haired woman laughed at something. Her pale skin a complement to the delighted flash of her whiskey eyes. Ryan glanced away, unnerved by the way his heart slammed at the sound of her laughter. Or was it her presence beside his mother? Sattler versus Laxalt.

His mother's dark eyes sought his. For a moment, she said nothing. Olivia busied herself with settling a sign in one corner of Papa Don's store window. "Miss Olivia and I will be fine. We will get much work done, and she will return me to the ranch this evening."

"I'll come get you."

Josephine's chin came up. "There is too much work to do on the ranch. You will listen to your mother in this."

His anger came hot, but he would not argue. Not here, in hearing distance of the Sattler woman. When he lifted his gaze, her eyes were on him. His mother took a step closer to Olivia and smiled at her as if they'd been friends forever. Confused by his mother's rejection, Ryan lifted the reins to back the horse up when he heard Olivia's words. "I'm so sorry."

He stilled, jaw clenched. Silence roared in his ears. He turned. She stood by the wagon alone, sunlight glinting against her face. The apology was for him alone. She took a step forward, eyes pleading. "I know I can't bring your father back, but you must believe I have no knowledge of…anything of my father's dealings. He's—"

Her voice broke, and she averted her face, the crisp outline of her jaw showing her struggle for composure. "It's like he's a stranger to me."

Her words hit him worse than a bullet to his gut. Not because of any feelings of sympathy toward her, but because the truth of her words twisted too deep. His mother didn't realize what a stranger he was to her. The few letters he had sent home had been truthful accountings of the type of work he'd found himself engaged in after those first wandering years. And then the offer had come to make real money.

"I want to find the truth," she said. "Tell me what you know, and maybe we can piece things together."

More words. These were soaked with sincerity. Her very presence twisted his insides and made him want to believe. Ryan withdrew from her gaze and focused on the window at her back—and at the small sign she had just placed there. Josephine Laxalt, Dressmaker. Inquire Within.

Ryan tightened his fists and turned away. "Sometimes it's better for a man to ride alone."

Josephine's dark eyes were on Olivia as soon as she entered the store. She didn't ask what had transpired between them, but Olivia could see the question in her eyes. Troubled more than she liked by Ryan's parting words, Olivia knew the man meant to do something. Soon. Revenge seemed such a harsh thing, but convinced as he was that her father had had something to do with the death of Martin Laxalt, or even that Jay Sattler was the one who pulled the trigger... .

"If you want to choose between these colors"—Josephine wrestled the bolts of chambray onto the section of counter Papa Don had allotted her—"we'll be done with all this."

Olivia reached out and cupped her hand over the older woman's. Josephine's dark eyes snapped to hers.

"He's hunting my father, isn't he?" She held the woman's gaze, waiting for the least flicker of guilty knowledge.

Josephine's shoulders slumped. "He is a good boy, but he cannot accept what is beyond his control."

"And what is that?"

The older woman tried to withdraw her hand. "We are friends. I—"

"If my father has done something wrong… If he is guilty of this thing, this murder, I must know." She swallowed. Disbelief raged in her mind. Her father would never shoot another man. Ryan Laxalt was crazy.

Josephine's shoulders quivered. "I do not know what your father has done. I know my husband is dead. Shot by a man who remains faceless. How can I accuse him of a deed that I did not see?"

"Your son seeks the truth."

Josephine's eyes closed. "He is full of anger. But anger makes you blind."

"You don't want to find out who killed your husband?"

Something cold and fearful tightened Mrs. Laxalt's features. "I fear the finding will get him killed."

Olivia digested those words. "I can't believe that my father would kill anyone."

"It is often hard to believe the worst of those we love."

"Your son—was he not with your husband when all this happened?"

"He returned after his papa was killed. Ryan has been away these past years. He left before your mama took sick."

Hard as she tried, she could not remember Ryan Laxalt as a boy. Not from socials or church or any other town events. But her world had been narrow as a child, and she expected there was much she had been oblivious to.

"He was a Texas Ranger for many years," Josephine said. Olivia did not miss the small smile of pride Josephine allowed herself. "Brought down many bad men."

Olivia recalled her uncle talking about Texas Rangers, Indians, and the outlaws they brought down. He'd been fascinated with all things West, and Olivia had often thought that if he'd had his druthers, he'd leave Aunt Fawn, move from Philadelphia to the West, and never look back.

She didn't know whether the fact was directed at her as a warning or as a passing comment meant to showcase a mother's pride in her son. Whatever the reason, Josephine said nothing more. She bent her head to the task of cutting yardage, her hands whisking wrinkles from the fabric as she cut.

Chapter 9

Directly after her fitting, Olivia went to the newspaper and tried to engage Marv in a conversation on the whereabouts of Tom Mahone. Maybe he had picked up news of the Laxalt murder and the underlying tension in the territory.

Marv's world seemed focused around placing paper onto an easel of sorts. Olivia watched the man in silence, mesmerized by the machine itself, if not the man's focus on his work. Marv glanced up at her before taking down two sticks with a thick blackened pad at one end. She saw why the brown end was stained when Marv moved to a tray and daubed a bit of stiff black ink on the ends. With movements sure and fast, he worked the paste between the ends of the sticks until it was smoother; then he patted it onto a tray of letters. He lowered the easel with the paper onto the tray and shoved it beneath a large, heavy-looking section. He pulled a handle once, then again, and rolled the platform back out. When he peeled the easel section back from the tray of letters, Olivia gasped at the wonder of seeing the process to make a printed paper.

As many times as she had read the papers in Philly or enjoyed the books, she had never seen the process. "How wonderful!"

Marv lifted the paper from the easel and held it carefully, brows knit.

Olivia slipped over to see the paper he held. "Will you show me how to do that?"

For the first time, Marv looked right at her, his hazel eyes were sharp, even hard. "Not for a woman. It's messy work and hard."

"I could help put the paper in the easel thing—"

Marv turned away and stepped toward a rack with other papers spread across it. Frustrated with the man's terseness, she was tempted to turn and leave, but she worked here now, and she might as well get used to Marv's silence—and he might as well get used to her presence.

A little desk in the corner suited her purposes for the present, but without Tom's guidance, how would she know what to write about? She went to the pages hanging along a drying rack. Dozens and dozens. They all seemed the same, but deep into the rows, she found a page that wasn't. The paper was dry, and the date was from a month ago. The editor was listed as Jon Pembroke. She read the articles, little tidbits of town news, but it was the column on page two that bit deeply into her heart. Her father's name appeared then disappeared beneath a layer of other names. Names she remembered from childhood. They were referred to as barons on the pages before her, and the writer was linking them to the death of a man. Bolder than the rest of the article was the notice right below it, posted by her father and spouting a warning that rustling from the big ranches would not be tolerated and would be dealt with swiftly.

Marv was suddenly there beside her, his hand on her arm. "I'll take that, miss. Mr. Mahone wouldn't want you to have seen this."

She whirled on him. "Why?"

"It's Jon's words. They didn't quite see eye to eye on things."

"Jon?"

"The old editor. Loved this paper and working for the town."

"He's—he's…dead?"

Marv shrugged, but he wouldn't look at her. "Left town real fast. Mr. Mahone's the editor now."

"What do you know about this?" She pointed to the article on the second page. "About this murder."

"Sheriff Bradley never arrested anyone. Said there was evidence only that George had rustled from Bowman's ranch, discovered during the roundup."

"Did you know the man?"

"The sheriff?" Marv grimaced. "Not much of the law in that man, if you get my meaning."

"I meant the man accused of rustling."

"Knew George real well. Good man. Trying hard to make a living. It's not right—" He stared down at his feet. She waited for him to finish.

"I've said too much."

"But it's not right for a man to steal another man's cattle, right?"

Marv held her gaze, eyes pinpricks. He held out his hand for the paper. "No. Now if you'll just let me have that…"

Olivia surrendered the sheet. Marv's dialogue was the most he'd ever said to her. His barely constrained anger was evident even in the way he walked, each step more a stomp. It didn't seem like a good time to introduce herself so he would stop calling her "miss" either, but being faced with more evidence that her father, and some of the big ranchers, were not held in high esteem added to her already troubled mind.

Olivia wandered out onto the street before she formulated what she could do, if anything, with the information. Where was Tom Mahone in all this, and were George's murder and the Martin Laxalt "rustling" charges related somehow? Landry's was busy when she stepped inside, but Phoebe took one look at her face and motioned her through the dining room to the kitchen. Her friend's hand on her shoulder directed her to a chair. Cold lemonade was pressed into her hand. She sipped at the drink, watching the owner's blurred movements as he expertly cooked and filled orders. His nod in her direction was the only acknowledgment of her presence.

Olivia processed the article again. The realization that her father's warning might have led to George's and Laxalt's deaths was sickening. Her mother would have been appalled and, had she lived, never would have allowed her husband to go to such lengths to protect his interests.

"You look pale as the moon."

Olivia blinked and raised her head. Phoebe's wan smile gave her courage. "I just read an old paper from a month ago about a man's death. George was his name. But there was something else, too. My father had penned a warning against those bent on rustling." She tried to formulate the question that rose in her mind about the whole thing—the simmering anger of Marv and the sudden departure of the old editor coupled with the deaths of two men.

Phoebe glanced over her shoulder. "I'll be back for the lunch crowd, Mr. Landry."

Her friend motioned her to follow. Olivia got to her feet and followed Phoebe up the back steps to her apartment. She made herself comfortable in the same chair she'd sat in on her previous visit, and her eyes searched the face of the woman in front of her—the angle of Phoebe's shoulders, the lines beside her eyes. Olivia's fingertips went cold. With a mixture of dread and acceptance, she realized that the emotion on Phoebe's face could only be identified as anger. And she thought she knew whom the anger was directed at.

Ryan knelt beside the gate. Traces of the crime were long gone, but he'd still returned to the spot where Bobby Flagg, foreman of the Laxalt ranch, had discovered the body of his father. Because of his worry over his mother and attempts to keep a firm hand on the roundup—no, he admitted, because of his anger at the deed—he'd allowed himself to believe his father a victim. Now, touching the very dirt that he imagined held vestiges of his father's spilled blood, Ryan wondered if it was possible that his father had rustled cattle. That had been the accusation. Laxalt head counts had been up in spite of the hard winter of 1886–87 and the drought of the previous summer. Bobby had assured him that his father had worked hard to bring water in from the low-lying, spring-fed pond at the far end of the Lazy L.

Ryan's spine stiffened. The gate where he stood was about half a mile from that pond. Thirsty Sattler cattle could have smelled the water and bunched against the fencing, doing damage in their desperation for a drink. He swung into the saddle and debated. He could look at the fencing around the pond or he could talk to Bobby.

It took him an hour to find the foreman, but when he slid from the saddle, Bobby was there with a ready grin on his ruddy face.

"Cody and Ty are working ten head from the brush down there. Got their hands full."

Sweat streaks showed on the man's face. He helped it along by smearing the back of his leather-clad hand across his forehead, leaving a dark stripe of dirt.

"Looking like we can head out in a few more days."

Ryan nodded slowly, pondering Bobby's words. "Sounds good," he said, "I wanted to ask you something about that pond. Place where you found—" He squinted into the sun and swallowed over the bulge of emotion wedged in his throat.

"Pond was a major player summer of '86. Only place that had any water at all. That it was on Laxalt property nettled everyone. Sattler and Bowman both tried to claim it was theirs before that summer, but they got downright nasty about it when the drought hit. Let their cows push against the fence and break through. Me and Martin finally realized we'd always have to maintain a hard patrol on that section."

"Was he patrolling when he got shot?"

"No. Not that far away from the pond. Ty was over there

that night. Said he heard a shot but thought it was one of Sattler's men shooting a critter of some sort. They'd been doing it throughout the day."

Bobby shifted in the saddle. "Me and the men went into town the other night for a drink and to look over the crowd for hands to hire. Heard some talk about you."

Ryan gave a stiff nod. "Expected as much. Whatever's said, just don't let my mama hear." Josephine Laxalt would prefer to think of her son as honorable.

Bobby inclined his head. "I was hoping it might help tame Sattler and Bowman some."

Ryan doubted it, and he already knew what Bobby's opinion of the big ranchers was; they'd discussed it as soon as Ryan had arrived on the ranch. Everything congealed into a ball of frustration, tight and hard, deep in his stomach. He gripped the reins and funneled his rage into action. "Need an extra hand?" He was already turning the mustang toward the hollow where his men struggled to bunch the cows.

"Sure, boss. Can always use an extra hand."

Chapter 10

"I'll be leaving town shortly. Starting up a little ranch of my own over by Bowman's. He's already given me trouble."

Olivia tried to process all that Phoebe was saying. Her friend would be leaving Buffalo. To start her own ranch. Alone?

Phoebe's eyes took on a glint. "I'm partnering with Jacob Isley. He's got himself a little house out there already. It was my idea to use his land for cattle. He's wanting to farm it, but I convinced him otherwise."

"You're marrying him?"

Phoebe pursed her lips. "I'm not the marrying sort. At least not yet. Might settle down someday. But that piece of land is big enough to hold us both, and there's an outbuilding where Jacob's already set up his things."

Olivia opened her mouth.

Phoebe crossed to her, and the anger came back into her expression. "Bowman's not playing nice. He's already threatened Jacob. Your father was out there with him one day, trying to convince Jake to take the buyout he was offering. A generous sum, but we aren't aiming to sell and move just because someone was getting too big for their britches and thinking we should."

"You said my father wasn't a nice man."

Phoebe plucked at the material of her skirt. "They've gotten clannish. Going around small ranches and making all kinds of accusations."

"But…why?"

Phoebe didn't respond. She crossed to a table and began yanking pins from her hair. It fell around her shoulders in a stream that she brushed with long, languid strokes. Olivia met her eyes in the mirror, begging her friend for an answer.

"It might be best"—Phoebe twisted her hair and inserted a pin—"if you use that reporting job to do some serious reporting."

Olivia couldn't grasp what Phoebe meant.

Her friend sighed and set the brush aside, facing her. "Tom Mahone is on their side and was hired to skew public opinion against small ranchers. Maybe he thinks by hiring you, you'll report what he wants you to."

"Why would he think that? He doesn't know me." Indeed, their talk had been superficial at best during the journey west.

"He knows you're a Sattler."

Ryan leaned against the mustang's heaving side and uncinched the saddle then rubbed along the place where the cinch strap had lain. The horse's hard run had done him good— made him feel alive in a way he hadn't since coming to Buffalo, or since finding out his father was dead. No, murdered. He needed to remember that.

Bobby, Ty, and Cody had retired for the evening, joking about how to prepare the fat rabbit Ty had shot into the dust on their ride back from the west field. The men were dusty and tired but in good spirits and confident of the fact that the really hard work was almost done.

Ryan wanted to join them. They shared laughs as they built a small fire to roast the rabbit on, and he felt the pull to shed the yoke of responsibility and eat with them rather than en-

dure the too-polite conversation, or even the pervasive dis-
agreements, eating with his mother would offer.

The rattle of a distant wagon brought him alert. The men,
too, heard it and turned to scan the horizon. Bobby's steps
took him a few paces into the clearing where he could get a
better view of the approaching people. Ryan interpreted the
hard look Bobby sent his way. His foreman feared his father's
murderer might be coming back.

He crossed to the man. "Not in a wagon. They'd be on
horseback." He knew who was in the wagon and sought to
further reassure Bobby. "My mother insisted on riding back
here with that Sattler woman."

Bobby's shoulders relaxed, and he let out a low whistle.
"Heard she was back. She was just a sprout when she left.
Took her mama's death real hard." The man shrugged and
turned away. "Not sure how to feel about having her here."

Ryan didn't miss the irony of his mother riding with a Sattler, and neither did the men. Wasn't that the whole reason
he'd cautioned her against whatever friendship she was de-
veloping with Olivia? "I'll make sure this is the last time she
feels welcome here."

Bobby stopped, his broad back a barrier. "Whatever your
mama wants is okay with me." He turned his face in profile,
and his words drifted over his shoulder. "Olivia Sattler is a
pretty one, but she's a Sattler just the same."

Chapter 11

Ryan was at his mother's side as soon as Olivia brought the wagon to a halt. He reached up to help his mother down, not oblivious to the smile on her face that wilted as soon as she saw him. He hated to think his mother might actually be enjoying Olivia Sattler's company while dreading his.

"Now go help Olivia down."

"No need." He let the words sink in, and waited for Olivia's whiskey eyes to meet his. "She won't be staying."

"I invited her for supper, Ryan."

He clenched his jaw tight, disgusted. His mother's hand touched his elbow and squeezed hard against his biceps. He never would have thought she possessed such strength in her hands.

"You can eat with the men tonight."

It was her own brand of rejection. A standoff of wills. She would not back down from befriending Olivia, and he would not back down from insisting she was the enemy. What played out in Olivia's expression caught him square in the chest. She lowered her eyes and picked up the reins. Her left hand drifted to release the hand brake she had just set. Every line of her body seemed cowed with disappointment. Just once she glanced his way, and he saw the sheen in her eyes. His mother's hand left his elbow as Olivia lifted the reins.

"I'll eat with the men," he said, and spun on his heel, away from the conflicting emotions stirred by these two women. Factions that should be at war with each other but insisted on pulling a blanket of peace over a crime. He would not do that. Could not. And hadn't he wanted to eat with the men anyhow?

A shift in the planes of Josephine's face flickered disappointment then resolve as she stared after her departing son. Olivia reset the brake, unsure what to say or how to think. Words seemed such a waste in the face of this conflict. She could see why Ryan would be angry and why his anger would extend to her, but she also felt regretful that he would keep her at arm's length without giving her a chance.

Throughout the simple meal, Josephine absorbed all that Olivia shared on fashion trends and city life. But it was hard to miss the plaintive glances the woman sent toward the front door as darkness descended. He was all she had in the world, and Olivia felt responsible for the grief her presence brought to their relationship.

Between clearing the table and wiping the last fork dry, Olivia made up her mind. "I'd like to go talk to Mr. Laxalt."

Josephine flinched. "My son, you mean."

"Yes."

"He will not talk to you."

"He might listen to what I have to say."

"What can you say to lessen the pain, Olivia?"

Olivia squeezed the towel she held. The baldness of the question surprised her. "Perhaps I can convince him that I am not his enemy."

"You bear the name Sattler."

She sighed. "Yes, I know. But you don't seem to hold that against me."

"I know your hands are clean of my husband's blood."

"Then I'll talk to him." She passed the towel to the woman, determined to bridge the gap between mother and son.

"Remember that our workers also see that you are first a Sattler, second a woman."

Hand on the door, Olivia's smile was tight. "But I am also your friend."

Chapter 12

Firelight flickered against the rough wall of the barn. Olivia's heart pounded, and her neck muscles were tight with worry. She changed directions, not wishing for her looming shadow to announce her presence. She would do this her way. She skirted the barn and came up the other side, directly in front of the house where the ranch hands bedded. Voices rose and fell with laughter. Words overlapped as the men tried to top each other with whatever wild stories they told. Horses seemed to be the subject from what she could comprehend.

She lingered at the corner of the building, telling herself she was not spying on the men. She wanted only to be prepared. One peek let her know the positions of the men around the fire. Ryan leaned back on an elbow, ankles crossed. Across the fire were two other cowhands, both sitting on wooden stumps. Empty plates were stacked at their feet, evidence that they had finished eating.

Ordering her thoughts, Olivia lifted her foot to step into the open but was stopped suddenly by the unmistakable click of a cocked hammer and a gravel voice at her back. "Never shot a lady before."

She spun, and a hand pushed her roughly against the rough poles of the building, pinning her. Pale eyes burned into hers.

The stranger's face was half in shadow, and firelight danced along the other side. She shuddered hard, for the man's face gave the impression of a demon come to life.

"Any reason for a woman to be poking around here, Mr. Laxalt?"

His overloud voice hurt her ears. She twisted to get free of his grip on her wrist. The looming figure of Ryan Laxalt appeared, and then the other two men came into view.

"My mother's guest, Ty. Let her go."

Ty seemed reluctant to obey, and his lips twisted in a sneer. "Your mother's guests always take to spying on people?"

Ryan didn't answer, but he nodded at the man beside him. "Bobby."

The larger man of the three seemed to interpret that message and motioned the other two men back toward the fire.

Olivia felt pinned beneath Ryan's dark eyes as she rubbed the place Ty had gripped. Prickles of fear and relief dueled for first place along her spine. "I wanted to talk... ." She stared at her feet and knotted her hands in the material of her skirts.

"Ty is keeping watch."

She raised a hand and rubbed the soreness of her wrist. She would have a bruise. "He does a great job."

His eyes flicked downward. "I'm sorry if he hurt you. Men are sometimes rougher than they realize, especially when threatened."

Her breath halted. When she searched his face, the darkness hid his emotion. But his choice of words—was he excusing himself? "I'm no threat."

"You're a Sattler."

"You can't think I'd have anything to do with your father's death. I just got here."

Ryan hesitated and stared into the darkness. A shot of wind ignited the fire, stripping the shadows from his eyes long enough for her to see the wariness.

She tried again. "Did you agree with everything your father ever did?"

* * *

Ryan said nothing. The answer was universal. Children never agreed 100 percent with their parents. He understood her point and admitted it to be a valid one.

"The accusation is that your father stole from mine." Her voice cut the silence. "Shouldn't we worry more about getting to the truth of the matter than standing here accusing each other based on loyalty? Neither of us was here when it happened."

"I do not condemn you for your father's mistakes."

She shifted and both hands worked along her upper arms as if warding off a chill. "Is that why you growl at me? Disapprove of your mother befriending me? Because I'm a stranger to Buffalo, and this is a display of western hospitality?"

Her questions plucked at that place down deep that remembered a man's responsibility of gentleness and respect toward a woman. Things were different in eastern cities, he knew. Especially among higher-class individuals. The proper male-female roles more defined. He'd hated his visit to New York, which had showed not only the lowest of the lowest class of people, but the highest of the high. The chasm between the two classes had sickened him. He did not wish to see the big ranchers crush the small. That event would make citizens of the West too much like those in the East. Yet his duty was clear. Miss Sattler deserved at least to be heard. "My apologies. My father and I did not agree on much, as I'm sure you and your father do not see eye to eye."

"My father is not the man I remember, Ryan."

Hearing his name fall from her lips in soft tones provoked a frown. Impatient, he jerked around and motioned. "Let's walk." He had no desire for his men to overhear whatever she had come to say.

Beyond the building and out of reach of the light of the fire, the moon guided his path toward the corral. He didn't turn to see if she followed, almost hoping that she did not.

"I want to help."

Her voice flowed over him, silent and entreating. He wondered if he could love her, and the suddenness of the thought rocked him off balance. He clung to the fencing surrounding the corral and lifted a booted foot to the bottom rung. His forearms scraped against the wood. The mustang came to him and nibbled at his sleeve, and still he could not answer her.

"Tom Mahone hired me to write for the *Buffalo Bulletin*."

Every part of his body felt the warmth of her presence as she appeared beside him. Her hand on his arm was placating, and he knew her eyes would be beseeching him to relent. "Tom Mahone is on their side from what I've been told."

Her breath whispered out on a sigh. "I…I need to know the whole story of your father's death."

"I'm sure your father would not approve of you teaming up with the enemy."

"You are not that, Ryan."

His throat closed at the gentleness of her statement "We're definitely not on the same side."

"Only because you have chosen what side you think I'm on, never considering that I am a mature woman with thoughts and opinions of my own. I am not afraid to align myself against my father, but…"

When she did not continue, he finally turned his head to her. A small smile played on her lips, though she wasn't watching him but rather stroking the mustang's side. He wondered why she felt so compelled to befriend his mother, or his mother to befriend her. It didn't make sense to him. He could not deny his curiosity. "But?"

She tilted her face up, the soft moonlight limning along her jaw and sparkling in her eyes.

"I want to print the truth. Not as my father sees it or even as you see it, but as things truly are. Both sides of the story. Maybe it will help one side better understand the other."

"I don't think Tom Mahone will like that too much."

She lifted her shoulders and sank her fingers into the mustang's mane. "I'll cross that bridge when I come to it."

Despite himself, he had to admire her spirit. He could even understand what it was his mother saw in the woman: a trait indefinable but indomitable. "So we are to work together?"

The question hung between them as she twisted a chunk of the mustang's mane around her index finger. She pushed away from the railing and brushed her hands together, her gaze meeting his. "I think that means we must first be friends. Don't you agree?"

Chapter 13

His eyes ran over her hair, auburn in the darkness. There was a straightforwardness about her that he liked, and his instinc rejected the possibility that her offer of friendship might be a trap. Nevertheless, he would be careful.

"I learned this afternoon that Phoebe was leaving Landry's She's moving out to a ranch beside Bowman's."

"Jacob Bowman," he said.

She nodded. "I remember him from a long time ago. He was a sourpuss."

"Still is."

"Have you always lived here? I mean, before you left."

He thought back to his restless feelings as a young man He'd worked the ranch beside his father, and his mother taugh him reading and arithmetic late at night. Not until he was ter did he realize a world existed beyond the Laxalt ranch.

"I left when I was fifteen."

"I don't remember you."

"You wouldn't."

The material of her dress rustled, and he glanced at her The tenderness in her expression caught his breath. "Tell me about your father."

He closed his eyes and swallowed, ordering his thoughts. "He was a hard worker."

"I can see that in your mother."

Of course she could. They had both poured so much of themselves into the ranch. Building it beyond their expectations and sacrificing so much in the process. Why was he only now able to see that? He'd chafed through his teens at the thought of hard work and sweaty palms, rope burns and trail dust. He'd hated it, and he'd taken that hate out on his father more than once. His father's impatience with him had erupted during a violent storm. Thunder and lightning had slashed the sky and rocked the world as driving rain pounded their bodies. They'd had to ride out into the pasture after Ryan's confession that he hadn't shut the gate. The young cattle might have spooked at the sound of the storm and run off a cliff.

He'd been so angry that night. So disgusted with having to go back out in the weather. Who cared about the cows? Didn't his father ever think of anything other than the animals?

Ryan remembered those burning thoughts that proved his immaturity. Even now he experienced a wave of bile at his foolishness. His father had had a right to be angry with him and his attitudes. But there was no use dwelling on it now, for he could turn back the hands of time no more than he could take back the bullet that stole his father's life.

"What about you?" he asked, wanting nothing more than to trounce the grief balling in his gut.

"My mother died, and my father thought it best that my aunt Fawn raise me. So I was bundled back east."

"How old were you?"

"Nine, but she'd been sick for months. It was harder right at the end. Daddy wouldn't let me in to see her."

What could he say to that? To have your mother die at such a young age must have been devastating.

"I remember praying to God every night to heal her…."

"Did you get mad when He didn't?"

Her eyes flicked to his. "Why, no. Of course not. I knew He had other plans for me."

"You accepted it"—he snapped his fingers—"just like that?"

Her shoulders rose on an inhale, and he could almost feel the grip of emotion that brought a glassy sheen to her eyes. He reviewed the question, angst bunching the muscles in his neck. He needed to know the answer for himself. For all his mother's talk of the Lord, of peace that passed understanding, he'd never felt it for himself. Never understood it or experienced it as his mother had—and now as Olivia claimed.

"I missed her, yes, but in my nine-year-old mind, my mother had taught me that God knew far more than we did about our future. She'd taught me to lean on Him when I didn't understand something. And—" Her voice faltered. She pressed a hand to her lips. "I knew that Mama would be in heaven and I would see her again."

"You make it sound so simple."

"It is simple. As a child. It's the grown-up ideas and experiences that muddy the water of faith."

He massaged his forehead and felt the cold sweat along his brow. God had been little more than a nuisance to him for so many years. Now the cold deeds of his hired-gun days scorched a trail against his conscience. *You've never done anything to regret.*

"Your mother is so proud of you being a Ranger."

He could not look at her. "I've not been a good man." A mild description, to be sure. But he could not bare his heart to her. To God, but not to her. Some sins cut to the bone.

"I guess this conversation means we're friends." She flashed a smile.

She'd taken him by surprise. Her candor, her kindness. Even glimpsing the light of her faith had warmed the cold places of his heart. She stirred his curiosity, and he could not deny the help she would be in getting at the truth behind his father's death. For the first time, he was willing to dig deeper than his assumption that Jay Sattler had fired the gun.

Olivia walked back to the wagon alone. Ryan had stayed behind at the corral. She thought she understood. Decision made, he needed to put distance between them, and though Olivia would be the first to admit she had little experience with men, she thought Ryan Laxalt might be fearful of working with her. His reluctance didn't make sense, though, and she shook her head as she released the brake and got the wagon rolling toward home.

Home. The word taunted.

Talking of her mother had felt natural and good, but calling the Sattler ranch house home left her cold and lonely. When she pulled up to the hill overlooking her father's house, her heart froze in dread. To enter those empty walls and pretend conversation with a man who mumbled answers and seldom smiled... If not for the need to be on horseback instead of in the wagon to do it, she would shoot off into the vastness surrounding the house and disappear. The idea did tempt though. But her father would expect her to be there and probably even now wondered what was keeping her so late. She wondered if her mother had ever felt such a disconnect—like her presence was merely a warm body in the house to her husband rather than a person with wants and needs, emotions, and a heart to share.

It shouldn't be like this.

As Olivia sat in the dark and stared at the house, her throat thickened and burned. Every bit of her rebelled against the idea of going into that loveless home to spend time with a man who barely knew she existed and didn't seem to care whether she was here or back in Philadelphia.

The horse dipped its head and curved its neck to look back, ears pricked. She heard the approach of a horse and rider and stiffened in the seat, but the sound stopped suddenly. Olivia gasped and darted a glance over her shoulder, trying to pinpoint the movement. A dark shadow moved closer. "Miss Olivia?"

Though he whispered, she recognized the deep voice as that of her new friend. She could make out the sweeping breadth of his shoulders and the glint of his dark hair in the pale moonlight.

"Is all well?" Ryan's whispered question reflected the concern in his face.

She saw his eyes dart between the house and the outbuildings. She couldn't help but feel touched by his presence. "I was just going in."

"You were still for too long. I thought you might be ill."

"You followed me?"

His teeth shone in the silver light. "I did. Riding this late at night is dangerous, even for a man. My mother would never have forgiven me if I hadn't made sure you were safe."

"Oh."

"Now that I know you are well, I'll be going before…"

He did not need to finish. They both understood the risk. He drew the reins up, bringing his horse's head around to turn the animal in a tight circle.

A swell of loneliness, maybe even pity, rose. If only she could go home with him and bask in the friendship she'd found with his mother. They could cook and talk and… "Ryan, wait." He stopped the horse and wheeled the animal broadside.

What could she say? He would not understand, and she wasn't sure she wanted him to. Her mind raced for an excuse to cover the impulsive words on the tip of her tongue. "Tomorrow. Maybe we should… I mean, could you show me around? I'd like to meet people, learn the names of some of our neighbors. We could meet in town and ride out to neighboring ranches. Someone knows something about your father's death."

She couldn't quite see all the details of his expression, but she thought she heard a smile in his tone. "It will help you with your article writing."

The front door of the ranch house opened. "Olivia?"

Ryan raised his hand and dug his heels into his horse's sides. The animal lunged forward, gained its footing, and settled into a gallop.

She set the wagon into motion. Her father waited until she pulled the horse to a stop. His hand touched her elbow and aided her descent. "Sorry I'm late."

"Was somebody with you?"

"A neighbor, making sure I got safely home."

If her father suspected anything amiss, he didn't question. "Been waiting supper for you. Got some leftover beans on the stove and a biscuit. You get on inside; I'll put the horse up."

Olivia raised on her toes and kissed his cheek. "I missed you, too, Father." Before he could form a response, she hustled past him and into the house.

Chapter 14

The sun beamed down unmercifully. Ryan's mother had insisted he take an extra hat for Olivia to wear when they went out for their ride. He now wished he'd never said a word about Olivia's request. His mother treated it like the official announcement that they were courting. Even as he dropped her off at the general store that morning, she'd trilled and chattered and moved with such a light step and quickness that he knew her hopes were soaring. Probably itching to knit baby booties.

He did his best to ignore all her mama-flapping ways, but when she eyed his head critically then asked him to bend down, her attempt to smooth down his cowlick right in front of the general store for all to see was the last straw.

"Never could tame that patch of hair," she groused.

He stuffed back his embarrassment, hoping the red-hot heat on his neck wouldn't climb higher. Ryan did his best to remain stone-faced, imagining the stares of a thousand townspeople spearing into his back and smothering grins of laughter. Bad enough he had to bring his mother into town, but for her to make a spectacle of him as if he still wore short pants and suspenders...

He adjusted the hat on his head lower over his eyes and hauled himself into the wagon. He left the conveyance at the livery and paid for the use of a dun. The Wyoming sunshine beat down hot on his shoulders, but the breeze against his face from the forward momentum of the dun eased the sweats. He and Olivia had never discussed what time to do the tour, cut off as they'd been by her father's appearance. As he made his way down Main Street, he figured he'd duck into Landry's and the newspaper office to see if Olivia was in town.

Landry's came up first.

Phoebe greeted him with an index finger pointing at an empty table in the corner and a nod of the head. The woman had her hands full in what was either a late-breakfast rush or an early lunch. No, too early for lunch he decided as he slid into the chair. At least from the table he had a clear view of the street and the comings and goings of people. Should Olivia pass, he could meet up with her and put a time on their planned ride.

Phoebe brought him water and dashed away when he held his hand up to indicate he wanted nothing else. When the crowd had dwindled somewhat, she slumped into the chair across from him. "I'll be so glad to be out of this place."

"Don't let Robert hear you."

She snorted. "He'll have someone to take my place before the door shuts behind me." Phoebe plucked at her apron and drew in a deep breath.

"You're leaving?" He recalled Olivia saying something about it.

"Got a place outside of town. By Bowman's. Me and Jacob Isley are hooking up to run it."

Ryan nodded. Jacob Isley wasn't a man he remembered, but he could see Phoebe hitching up with a rancher. "You know much about what's going on 'round these parts?"

"You mean the shooting of your father." It wasn't a question, and the way her eyes hardened told him she knew quite a bit on the subject. She tugged a rag from the pocket of her apron.

"Seems Sattler is getting too big for his britches."

"He's sure not the affectionate type. Olivia's hurting something awful. He's turned cold since his wife's…" She clamped her mouth tight and gave a little shake of her head. "But I guess that affects Olivia more than it does you."

If Olivia was hurting over something, Phoebe was right, it wasn't any of his business. "Olivia and I are supposed to ride around the town. She wants to meet her neighbors."

Phoebe had been rubbing a chunk of hardened yolk off the table when her head jerked up. "You and Olivia?" Her brow knit. "Riding around where?"

"Is something wrong with that? You thinking we might need a chaperone?"

Phoebe returned to the yolk, alternately scraping at the sunny patch with her nail and rubbing over it with a damp cloth. "Could arouse some talk, but I don't expect talk will worry Olivia. Or you for that matter."

"Got a mind to ride around myself. Check out Sattler's property more thoroughly, especially that section that butts up to our ranch."

Phoebe tugged at the lobe of her right ear. Her tongue darted out over her lips, and she would not meet his eyes. "Just be careful. Keep Olivia safe."

She didn't give him a chance to ask for an explanation before she scraped the chair backward and hurried toward the kitchen. Conversation over.

When Olivia emerged from the general store garbed in her first new piece of western clothing, a riding skirt, she felt like she had finally shed her city-girl ways. It felt good. As soon as she opened the door to the *Bulletin*, Marv's gaze caught hers then lowered to the floor. At least now he would look at her. Tom rose from the desk at the back of the room and motioned her forward. His smile stretched from ear to ear. Hair pulled back taut and wet with a generous amount of hair oil, Tom Mahone looked every inch a charming personality, except for the dark shadow of his eyes and the scar on his right cheek.

"Mr. Mahone."

"Olivia. I've been meaning to speak with you. How are you coming on your first article? It's due Friday, as I'm sure Marv has told you."

Tom's eyes slid to Marv, and she didn't miss the way the older man responded with slack-jawed amazement.

She bided her time forming a response. Thick tension buzzed in the room. "I haven't been in very often," she said, eyes on Marv. Did she imagine the release of tension in his thin shoulders?

"I see." Tom leaned forward, the squeak of his chair loud in the room. "I don't tolerate lateness, Olivia, and I won't accept just anything to run in this newspaper."

His smile was fashioned to take the sting from his words, she was sure, but his message came through loud and clear. If she did not write what suited his tastes, her articles would not be run, and she could be fired. He leaned forward, and she braced herself.

"Have you thought any more about having dinner with me?"

Olivia lunged upward, disgusted by the man's taciturn personality. Though she'd never met the editor of the Philadelphia newspaper, there had been no such pressure to report styles according to the fashion editor's taste. And that was the difference she realized. This wasn't the city where several editors headed different sections of the newspaper. The *Buffalo Bulletin* was run by one man, and she must not forget that. Attractive though he might be, she did not approve of the way he shifted and twisted to fit his own purpose.

She started for the door, calling over her shoulder. "I bid you a good day, Mr. Mahone. I'll have my article on your desk Thursday." There. Take that.

"Miss Sattler." She could tell by the squeak of his chair that he was on his feet. Next thing would be a protest from him, something calculated to smooth matters over. She didn't stop to listen.

Chapter 15

Ryan called himself every kind of fool for sitting around doing nothing while waiting on a woman. The dun stood three-legged at the hitching post, dozing in the heat of the afternoon sun. He was paying good money for the horse, and here he sat. Doing nothing. Waiting on a woman who might or might not show up in town just because she asked to ride with him. His brain was becoming as brittle as a cow pie in the sun.

Phoebe checked on him one more time, probably hoping he would just leave. With the beginnings of lunch, the crowds would explode, and she would need his table. He would check the paper's office. Decision made, Ryan flicked a coin onto the table and stretched to his feet. Dust hung in the air outside the restaurant, residue of the passage of a fast-moving wagon down Main. He unhitched the dun, who seemed uninterested in anything other than staying right where he was.

He glanced once more at the office of the *Buffalo Bulletin*. A slender form ducked from the newspaper office. Soft strawberry hair, a delicate complexion… His heart beat harder at the sight of her, and he kicked the dun into motion.

"Been looking for you." He wished the words back as soon as they left his mouth. He sounded like some pathetic sop. Leaning forward, he rested his hands on the pommel and finally noticed the thin line of her lips and the dangerous flash pulsing from her eyes. Though she stopped, she acted as if she hadn't heard a word he'd said. Good.

"Something wrong, Miss Sattler?"

Her skirt skimmed along the road, and her feet left a small trail of smoky dust with every step that drew her closer to him. "I can't wait to get out of this town and get some work done on my first article."

He covered his grin as she scurried up into her wagon and backed the horse up. He enjoyed seeing her rankled. He bet Tom Mahone was just now realizing what a spirited filly he'd employed. But how she figured on exploring rough terrain in a wagon was beyond him.

"I'll drop the wagon off and get a horse. Daddy left a list of some things to pick up," she said. Her words came out like an explosion of buckshot. "I'll meet you at your place."

Whatever emotion had her in its grip, it sure wasn't the joy of riding with him that he'd hoped to elicit. Still… "Sounds good to me." He turned the dun as she struggled to back the horse.

"Harder to learn a wagon than a saddle," he said as he dismounted. He put a toe on the step up and hesitated. She grinned, put the reins down, and slid over to make room for him.

"Lesson number one. Make sure you put even pressure on the reins. The horse'll know how to back up, but he needs some time."

She took in his words and ways, studying how he handled the reins as he backed the wagon far enough away that she would be able to turn out onto the main road. Without another word, he handed the reins to her and jumped down. He lifted his head, and one side of his mouth curled upward. "You look nice. Just like you never left Buffalo."

"Your mother's doing. She's going to make a name for herself in this town."

"Not all her doing." And this time she saw the appreciation in his eyes. He lifted his brows and winked, and she felt her blood warm at the attention.

"You, sir, are a flirt."

Ryan didn't respond. He was too busy settling himself in the saddle. He motioned her forward and allowed the dun to fall into step alongside the wagon, far enough back that she would have to turn to see him.

It took her some time at the stable to find a hand available to saddle a bay mare that looked gentle. The hand worked slow enough that she could follow his moves as he settled a blanket on the horse's back then threw the saddle on and put a belt around its belly that reminded her of a corset. As he gave her a hand up, she was grateful that her father didn't appear to ask where she was headed.

Ryan was at the place where the Rocking S touched Laxalt property. His back was to her, and he held the reins of his horse loose in one hand. She studied his silhouette until the beat of her horse's hooves alerted him to her presence and he turned.

"Are you ready, cowboy?"

When his gaze met hers, a smile creased the corners. It softened the hardness in his face.

"You should smile more often. It makes you look younger, gentler."

"Since when is a man supposed to look gentle?" He turned and fiddled with something behind the saddle then held out a battered hat to her. "It'll keep the sun off your face."

She accepted the hat, chagrined that he might have noticed her freckles. The hat was big on her head and slid down over her eyes until she angled it back. "Don't most mothers want their sons to grow up to be kind and loving?"

He ran his knuckles along his cheek, and she followed the motion. "You've got me there, though too much of that can smother a man."

"Guess that's why God gives us a father and a mother. We learn different qualities from each."

The horses picked their way down a rock-strewn path that emptied into a grassy plain. A stream rushed through on its way to the horizon. They stopped their horses, dismounted, and let them drink. The quietness of the rangeland was comfortable, almost sacred. It seemed a shame to break it, but she had to ask the question uppermost in her mind.

In slow, measured moves, he helped her get back into the saddle then did the same. "Why do you think my father killed yours?"

He lifted his hat and pushed a hand through his hair. His lips formed a frown. "Some wire was cut." He moved the dun ahead of her bay. "I've no doubt my father saw that. My best guess is he confronted your father and came out on the short end of the stick."

"Couldn't it have been anyone? One of Daddy's ranch hands?"

"They work for him."

"Guilt by association?"

The edge in her voice showed what conclusion she was jumping to. Funny how after such a short time knowing her he could envision the clouds coming over her face. A beautiful face. Beautiful hair. She was dainty, and he wondered if she would feel fragile in his arms… .

Crushing his wayward thoughts, Ryan slowed the dun until Olivia came even with him. Sure enough, her expression was severe, and she looked just like a woman ready to bawl. Ryan adjusted himself in the saddle and cleared his throat. "Didn't we just settle this yesterday? Friends, I think, was the final offer."

"Good." She angled her face away from him and tilted the broad brim of her hat to further obscure her face. "But sometimes we're going to have to ask each other hard questions. We should be ready for that." She rested her hand against the pommel. "It could have been one of Daddy's ranch hands who took it upon himself to handle things."

Ryan wanted to protest but could not. Hadn't he just come to the same conclusion?

"Evidence is gonna be scarce," he said. "There's been too much rain, and too much time has passed."

"Then we'll have to rely on people."

Rankled by her logic even as he was forced to acknowledge the soundness of it, Ryan stuck his hat back on his head. "Bobby saw the wires cut—"

"Who's Bobby?"

"My foreman."

"He saw the wires being cut, or he saw the cut wire? One indicates he saw the deed done, the other that he saw only the evidence."

Ryan closed his eyes, already lost in the labyrinth of her reasoning, no matter how sound it was.

"Our problem, Ryan, is we need facts. Someone knows who pulled the trigger. It's figuring out who knows what or who saw the deed done—that's the trick." She tossed him a look, all vestiges of vulnerability gone. This was the face of a woman with a task that needed done. "Before we go to the obvious people for help, let's ride north of here."

"That would be Hector Maiden's property."

"Big rancher or small?"

"A farmer mostly. A few head from what I've heard."

She nodded. "It's a place to start."

He'd lived a good portion of his life being directed by the whim of a man's belief in his own version of the truth. It had been a shot at a man who later turned out to be innocent that turned his stomach. An innocent man laboring under an accusation, only to be found innocent long after his body had grown stiff and cold.

She kicked her horse into motion. Left with little choice, Ryan got the dun moving, feeling his lead in this fight slipping through his fingers. Worse, it didn't bother him near as much as it should. Her lithe body seemed to take to the gait of the horse easily. No sir, it wasn't near so hard to follow her lead as he'd thought it might be.

Chapter 16

"They've shuffled their big boots all over my farm trying to stir up trouble."

Olivia nodded over the cup of coffee Hector Maiden had supplied. She'd let the farmer know right off who she was, that she wrote for the *Buffalo Bulletin*, and that she wanted to know the truth.

Hector obliged her, even though his coffee was weak and the slice of corn bread he offered looked like he'd had to scrape off the mold before putting it on a plate for her. Ryan sat across from her. He glanced at the corn bread then back at her, one eyebrow raised. He'd no doubt seen her reaction to the corn bread.

Hector sat at the head of the table, fingers drumming the surface with one hand, stroking the length of his bushy, yellowed beard with the other. "Don't own much, but what I have is mine." He made a fist and slammed it down on the table. "I don't aim to give it over to them just because Bowman thinks his cows might need a nibble of my corn."

Olivia nodded in agreement. "What about Martin Laxalt? You heard about—"

"Martin was a good man. Helped me get up the fence in the back for some cows. Reckon on starting to build a herd.

That'll stir a rattler's nest with Bowman." Hector barked a laugh that showed his teeth—or lack of them.

She snatched a glance at Ryan. She realized in the noise of Hector's diatribe just how quiet Ryan was by nature. A listener, her aunt would call him. Hurt lines traced a path between his brows, and she knew the mention of his father had twisted a fist in his grief.

"Do you know about the shooting?" Olivia asked.

Hector continued to chomp on his mustache. "Know what I heard. Sattler did the deed. Accused Martin of rustling his cattle. Two met out by that fence, and Sattler took the opportunity to pull the trigger. Reckon he thinks it's just a matter of time before Martin's widow packs up and leaves."

"They have a son," she said.

Hector bobbed his head. "Knew him when he was a lad. Left when he was a tadpole. Hotheaded. Grieved Martin something awful. Who knows? Might marry his widow myself. She's some kind of cook, and we could put our land together. That'd give Bowman and Sattler heart trouble for sure."

Olivia glanced at Ryan. His mouth was set in a firm line.

"Mr. Maiden"—Olivia pointed to Ryan—"this is Ryan Laxalt, Martin's son."

Ryan shot her a perturbed look.

"Well, why didn't you say so, son? Guess my marrying plans will have to wait then." Hector bellowed another laugh before his voice quieted a notch. "Sorry about your pa."

Olivia nipped the point off the corn bread and steeled herself against the dryness of the morsel and the thought of eating mold. It was all the man had to offer, and she wouldn't turn her nose up at it for anything.

She stabbed at the corn bread again and scattered the dry piece to make it look like she'd eaten more than she really had. A quick glance at Hector assured her he wasn't taking notice. But Ryan's eyes darted away the second she glanced his direction. He'd been watching her. The most minute tilt of his lips said it all.

Mischief stirred in her head, and she set her fork aside. "I don't think I can eat another bite." All eyes came to her. Giving Ryan her brightest smile, she slid the plate across the table to him. "Finish this up for me, won't you?"

Olivia breathed in the night air as she waited for Ryan to appear from behind Hector's cabin. She grinned up at the moon. Her horse shifted its weight, and she ran her fingers beneath its mane and scratched. When she finally heard the outhouse door moan a low creak and Ryan's boots rustling through the dry grass, she made sure to busy herself looking for something to help her into the saddle. The porch would have to do.

"I guess you're mighty proud of yourself."

She started at his nearness. Arching a brow, she clapped on the hat he'd let her borrow. It hadn't settled onto her head for more than a second before he whisked it off. She turned to face him. "Hey!"

He held it high over his head with one hand and put a finger to his lips with the other. "Unless you want Hector to talk all night, you'd better not let him know we're still out here. Besides"—he lowered the hat, his smile wide—"it's getting dark. There's no need for you to wear this."

He nested her hat inside his and tied them behind the saddle before mounting the dun.

"I suppose we can leave now." She couldn't resist the jab.

"Worst corn bread I've ever eaten."

"At least you were polite."

She led her horse over toward the porch and started around its head when she felt Ryan beside her.

"Need a hand?"

"I'll use the porch."

His arm snaked out around her waist, and she was yanked back against him. His hand clamped down across her mouth, and his voice was a hard whisper against her ear. "Someone's out there."

Her heart slammed. His hand fell, but she could feel his

tension. He left her in a rush, and she rocked on her feet for want of the support his body had offered. He went into a low crouch and moved forward a fraction. The night air moved in around her. She shivered.

Chapter 17

Ryan heard the noise again and settled his hand against the butt of his gun. Something was going on. He heard Hector's few calves moving and the sheep bleating, but he could see nothing.

He ducked around the back corner of the house where he could get a better view and still be in shadow. Glass shattered nearby, and a muffled curse rent the air as the barrel of a shotgun slipped through a back window.

Hector.

"Whoever's out there better get."

Flat against the house, Ryan knew Hector couldn't see him. He sidestepped until he could grab the barrel of the gun. "It's me," he whispered. "Ryan Laxalt. Someone's stirring your cows."

Hector's eyes were bleary, and his hair exploded from his head. "What you still doing here?"

Ryan put a finger to his lips and jabbed his head toward the door, indicating the man should come outside. He glanced behind him and retraced his steps to the corner of the house. Olivia stood there, his rifle in her hands. Seeing her preparation pleased him.

"I thought you might need my help. Was that Hector?"

"He's coming out. Let's get back to the horses and take a ride."

With Hector leading the way, they followed a worn path along the front section of his land where the new fence had been put up. The calves had calmed. His sheep were quiet.

Olivia had been silent the entire time. On occasion he would pull the dun in closer to her to gauge how she was doing. Her expression was always alert and intense. "It could have been a wild animal," she said. A thought that had already occurred to him.

Darkness was blanketing the hills when they finally left Hector's farm. Olivia came abreast the dun and smirked at him. "At least he didn't ask why we didn't leave right away."

"Or offer any more corn bread."

He liked the sound of her laughter, muffled as it was in light of the situation, and the way her hair flowed over her shoulders and down her back as she vented her mirth. He couldn't help but grin, and it felt freeing somehow. He'd become too serious. Perhaps too single-minded.

"Thinking about your father?"

Ryan sat up a little straighter.

"I think about my mother all the time. More now than when I was in Philly. I guess being here makes it more real. I can feel her here." She gave a little laugh and shrugged. "I'm sure I sound silly."

"No. You were sent away. It makes sense that coming back would stir everything up. Maybe you didn't have time to grieve. And now, God—" He paused. How long had it been since he'd directly referred to the heavenly Father? "God brought you back here for a reason," he finished, not even sure where such an idea had come from or if he even believed it. Olivia did. All he knew was the squeeze of his conscience made the weight of his past deeds unbearable. It seemed too easy a thing to shift the load to God and be done with it. Too easy for a man who collected money to murder. But only once. He gasped for breath as he saw the face of the man, twisted in pain.

Ryan looked over at Olivia, trying to forget. Centering his focus on her eased his guilt. Maybe God had a hand in bringing Olivia home to Buffalo. And maybe, just maybe, it was so that their paths could cross.

Olivia decided she liked Ryan without a hat. It made him seem less tough, more little boy. She wondered if he would get embarrassed if she gave voice to that thought or if he'd think her plain crazy. He might even get offended or angry.

In many ways, Ryan was a mixture of man and boy. Hector's observation about Ryan as a boy had revealed a crack in his tough-guy facade. Funny how she'd never figured him as someone quick of temper. Quiet, yes. Even brooding. But angry?

"God brought you back here, too," she suggested to his silhouette. His jaw worked for a few seconds before he met her gaze and nodded.

"I wish I'd come back sooner."

"You can't bring back your father, Ryan. He's gone."

It was there in an instant, the flash of temper. For all her conclusions about him, she could see that Hector had been correct. Yet there was something else, too, and she recognized it because it mirrored what she felt. Grief.

"My mother needs me."

"She's always needed you." Even in the short time she had known Josephine, Olivia saw her innate kindness and devotion to others. Now focused on her son. "I'm sure it hurt her terribly when you left. She's proud of you. You should have seen her smile when she told me you were a Texas Ranger for four years."

His quietness said a lot about him, whether he realized it or not. Olivia decided that Ryan's temper might have been quick once, but maturity had helped him learn to turn the anger inward in quiet reflection.

"Yeah, well, it wasn't quite like that."

She blinked up at him, confused.

"I worked for a Ranger once. Mentioned it in a letter. They hired me to track a man wanted in Texas and Oklahoma." His chest heaved. "I found him."

"You took him back to Texas?"

"Naw, he got wind that someone was on his heels. Makes a fella twitchy. He pulled lead on me, and I plugged him."

"But…"

"Purely self-defense." His gaze was searching. "You're surprised."

She said, "I mean, how did your mother think you were a…?"

He raised a shoulder. "Guess she read in the letter what she wanted to read. I worked for them for a few years doing odd jobs."

She mulled what he'd revealed about himself, surprised at his past. Shooting a man seemed such a brutal thing. Savage. When she sneaked a glance at his profile, she wondered how such blatant violence could thrive and what its presence meant for the future of the West. But shooting in self-defense—that had to be honorable and right.

They rode in silence except for the creak of the saddle, the plod of the horses' hooves, and the distant howl of a coyote. When they got to the gates of her father's ranch, she slid to the ground, hoping the walk would stretch her muscles and relieve some of the ache she knew she'd feel in the morning. She slipped the reins over her horse's head and turned toward Ryan.

He smiled. "We didn't get very far."

"No, we didn't. If it hadn't been for Hector's corn bread…"

He shrugged. "What can I say? I was trying to be considerate and help a lady out."

She burst into laughter. "Your mother told me you had a soft heart under all the 'crust,' as she put it."

He swung his long leg over the back of his horse and dismounted. "Then I shouldn't disappoint. I'll walk with you to the house."

"I don't know. My father…"

"He'll never see me."

She wanted to say no, especially after the earlier incident. "It's not necessary."

He made a face and put a hand over his stomach. "Neither was the corn bread, but I did it anyway."

She shook her head and gave up trying to dissuade him. He came near and held out his hand for the horse's reins. She surrendered them to his warm palm, more aware than she wanted to be of his height, the broadness of his shoulders, and the shadow across his face that hid his gray eyes.

"We should do this again."

He hesitated, and in that second her heart cantered with expectation and the longing to spend more time with this man. To know his heart as she had discovered the heart of his mother.

His tone came out hard. "Based on what Hector told us, you could be right. Others know another side of my father's shooting."

She released a heavy sigh. His father's murder. He still believed that her father had pulled the trigger. The only reason Ryan wanted to spend time with her was because she'd offered to help him get to the truth. She must not allow herself to think his motives might extend to anything more.

Chapter 18

Ryan felt himself drawn as if by an undertow toward Olivia Sattler. When her fingers had grazed his, he'd been distracted by the silver light across her cheek. She would fit into his arms quite nicely.

Madness. All of it. He had scrambled to set his mind on the right track, throwing out some blather about Hector and the possibility that she might be right to assume others could help them find the truth. Of course she was right. He'd become more convinced of that as he'd listened to Hector talk, but he couldn't help but consider how disappointed she must feel to know that despite Hector's help, the truth of his words still pointed a finger at her father.

He could not deny the thunder of his heart as his fingers caressed hers or the churn of softer emotions her closeness brought to the surface.

He led her horse, his mind clearing now that he wasn't distracted by the sight of her. An animal hadn't scared Hector's sheep; he was sure of it. "I'll spend the morning over at Hector's. That way I can satisfy myself by knowing whether it was animal or man out there tonight."

"Ryan." She stopped him with a hand on his arm, but she wasn't looking at him, and her body was tense.

A man stepped from the shadow of the barn. "Miss Sattler."

"Skinny, you startled me."

The foreman nodded his response and almost yanked the reins from Ryan's hands. The horse jerked back. "Heard you were in town, Laxalt."

Olivia's voice wobbled with uncertainty. "He was just seeing me home."

Skinny's hard, pale eyes raked him. "I'm sure Mr. Sattler will thank you for seeing his girl home. Now get out of here."

"I'm here for Olivia. Not for you."

"And I told you to get."

Olivia filled his vision as she wedged herself between them. "Leave Mr. Laxalt to me, Skinny."

Skinny ran a hand over his bare scalp. His hard frown turned his face mean. Without a word, he led the animal away, steel in his eyes. The man had too much sand to let Olivia have the last word on the matter.

Ryan clamped a hand on her shoulder, spinning her to face him. "Don't ever do that again." His words came out hard. Much harder than he'd intended.

"I think I just saved your hide, and you have the nerve to tell me 'Don't ever do that again.' What? Should I let him blow your head off next time?"

"He couldn't draw; he had the horse's reins in his right hand."

"You could just say thank you."

It had escalated far beyond what he'd intended. "Thank you." He clipped the words, sinking beneath the weight of them and the hurt and anger his rebuke had generated.

She shook his hand from her shoulder and walked away. Ryan felt a coldness at the loss of her presence and a deep shame. He knew she'd meant well, but a man didn't need a woman to fight his battles for him.

Seething over Ryan's insolence, Olivia found great satisfaction in slamming the door behind her, even as late as it was.

"Where have you been?"

She turned, searching through the darkness of the kitchen in front of her for the source of that voice. Her father moved, a shadow in the darkness. A light flared, and then the chimney of a lamp was lowered. Her father's face came into view.

"I was over at Hector Maiden's."

"Alone?"

"No."

"Tom told me he hired you to write for his paper."

The shift in subject caught Olivia off guard. If he knew, what did he expect from her? Confirmation seemed absurd. Surely he wouldn't demand she quit, stay home, and be a good little ranch girl.

Olivia crossed the room and sat down across from him. His gaze probed hers, questioning. She felt much like the schoolgirl in front of the class, asked a question that she did not know the answer to.

"I'm sure you'll do a good job. I've some ideas for a few stories."

So this is how it was to be. She lifted her chin. "As do I."

"I told Tom you would do a good job."

She filled her lungs with air and did her best to bite back the surge of anger and the tears that stung. "I've been here for weeks, and our first real conversation isn't anything about how glad you are that I'm home. It's just about me doing a good job working in town?"

"Reputation is everything."

"It's nothing if you're not human."

Jay squinted his whiskey-colored eyes, a mirror of her own. His mouth drew into a hard line. "That's no way to talk to your father."

"Is that what you are to me? A father?"

"Don't forget who paid for you to be with your aunt all those years."

"It wasn't my choice to go to Philadelphia in the first place. It was your choice, Father. The choice you made for me."

"You were happy."

"I was lonely."

"You adjusted."

Words dissolved on her tongue. She stood to her feet, trying to compose herself before the dam of her emotion burst. "I miss the days when you were a father and not a stranger. But it's been a long time. Perhaps too long."

As soon as she was out of the circle of light, she picked up her pace until she reached the sanctity of her room. There, in the darkness relieved by a ray of moonlight, Olivia sat on the edge of her bed and covered her face. Hot tears squeezed from her eyes in spite of the defiant fists that balled to hold them back. But the dam of her will did not hold. Pulling her knees to her chest, she rocked, wishing for nothing more than a loving hand or a tender touch.

Or Mama.

Chapter 19

Ryan tied the dun to the back of the wagon and waited at the side for his mother to appear. When she did, her smile beamed brighter than the light from seven oil lamps. She wanted details of his time with Olivia, so he knew she'd forgive him for spending the morning with Hector Maiden and taking her to town late.

"So you must tell me when you are going out next."

He groaned and thought about how Olivia had stalked away from him the previous evening. "I don't know. Probably not for a long time."

She touched her hand to his as she tamed her skirts with the other and hiked herself into the wagon. "You were a gentleman, I hope."

Ryan took his time rounding the wagon. He might as well continue to answer the endless string of questions. If he grew silent, she would only dig deeper, prying open his shell much as he'd seen a sailor do to a clam once. The image made things bearable somehow, and his mother's stream of speculation and advice over the few miles into town made one thing clear to him: she wanted grandchildren. Lots of them. And she loved him. Love, to her, translated to a life spent with someone. Only there was one problem, and he told her about it as soon as he'd helped her down into the street in front of the general store. "We're not in love, Mama."

She stopped, turned, and smiled. It was the grin of a woman sure of herself. "You will be, son. She's a beautiful woman."

"I thought you wanted me to marry for love, not for beauty."

"Ah"—she shook her finger at him—"see? You are admitting that you have noticed how pretty she is. You see, I was talking about her inner beauty. You, on the other hand, are the one who notices her outward beauty."

He didn't respond. He should have known better in the first place. His mother could twist things around until his mind felt frayed like a used rope. He felt as if he'd scaled the Big Horns by the time he'd returned the dun to the livery and started back toward the ranch. And all because a little scrap of a woman knew him better than she knew herself. He wondered if all mothers had a way of turning their children inside out.

Bobby wanted him to go over the books. A task he welcomed. He wanted to learn more about the holdings of the Lazy L and forget about women.

He slapped the reins against the horse's rump to hurry her along. He needed to give more attention to the ranch. At the Y in the road, the right branch led to Sattler's spread, the left to Laxalt land. He stopped the wagon and considered Olivia and their hasty parting. Phoebe's words that she thought Olivia might be hurting over her father's inattention stirred his mind.

Ryan blew out a breath and adjusted his hat more firmly on his head before setting the horse into motion at a good clip. A mile ambled by when he spotted a dust cloud in the distance and paused the wagon to squint. The rider was coming fast, the horse and rider a dark blur.

His hands tightened on the reins as the rider became identifiable. When Bobby Flagg stopped, his apple cheeks were red from exertion.

"Headed to get the sheriff." His breath came in pants. "Found cut fence on that piece between our property and

Hector's. Went to talk to Hector Maiden." Bobby hunched forward over the saddle.

"Easy, man."

Bobby shook his head. "Hector is beat up. Not quite conscious."

"Who's with him?"

"Cody. Ty was taking care of the fence."

"You get on to town. I'll get over to Hector's. Ask Phoebe if she can bring Mama home tonight."

Olivia's body sagged in the saddle. What had started as a glorious morning was quickly becoming a savage beast of heat. She fanned the material of her blouse and slid to the ground of Main Street. Tom Mahone was not in the office, and Marv sat at a desk. His long, thin face showed displeasure.

"Good morning."

"I had nothing to do with it," Marv said.

Olivia understood at once what the man referred to—the conversation with Tom the previous day and the veiled suggestion that Marv had told her about the article's due date.

"He says things like he told me to do them, but he didn't. I had no way of knowing anything about a due date. I just keep the machinery running around here. If he keeps pushing me, I just might quit. Shoulda left with Jon."

"I have my article right here." She slipped the papers from a leather clutch and unfolded them. Though the article spoke only of her impressions of Wyoming as a city girl coming west, it was a start. She had wanted to write about Hector Maiden's revelations but changed her mind at the last minute. She preferred to gather more facts.

Or maybe it was the dark frown on her father's face that burned in her imagination whenever she tried to put Hector's observations on paper.

"They don't want your opinions, Miss Sattler. They want someone who'll write what they want to print."

"I see that, Marv."

"Your daddy…"

She waited for him to continue, but he only pressed his lips together and returned his attention to a piece of metal sitting on the desk.

"Do you think he killed Martin Laxalt?"

Marv's look was hard for a second before his gaze fell to the desk again. "Martin was a good friend. Didn't deserve what happened to him. George neither." His gnarled hands skimmed the metal pieces in front of him. "There'll be others, too."

Coldness crawled along her spine. She didn't know Marv. Wasn't sure if the crusty old man could be trusted or even if her fears were something she should talk about. She'd heard so many people express negatives about her father, but she wanted to believe he was the man she remembered. Yet so many little things stirred her fears and concerns to the contrary. Marv's face was drawn into lines of concentration as he worked over the part he held. And she didn't know if she wanted to dig any deeper.

Chapter 20

The general store promised relief from the heat and companionship in the form of Josephine Laxalt. The Singer sewing machine whirred and sputtered in the corner of the store, and Olivia noticed a woman hovering at Josephine's elbow. It appeared that they were discussing the sewing machine's wonders.

"Ah, Miss Olivia," Papa Don greeted her as he waved good-bye to a departing customer. "Is today the day you receive the rest of the clothes Mrs. Laxalt has been sewing for you?" He wagged his finger as he shook his head. "I tell you, that machine is never silent when she is here."

"Good for business, I'm sure."

Papa's eyes sparkled. "Very good. Sold two of the new-fangled things since Mrs. Laxalt has set up shop in the corner." He leaned on the counter and cupped his face in one hand. "What can I do for you today?"

She lifted her gaze to the shelves filled with jars of candy and seeds and hesitated. "I'd like some…peppermints."

Papa Don straightened and lifted down the jar of candy. "How many?"

"I…" Her throat closed. Here was a man who'd known her all those years ago. More importantly, he knew her father and mother. She could still hear Mother's voice ordering the sweet. "A nickel's worth."

"Ah, you're your mother's daughter." He turned and scooped peppermints from the canister. "Your pa always ordered extra sugar for your mama to make fruit pies and cakes. Still does. Guess his cook has a sweet tooth, too."

Anxiousness rose up in her, and she blurted the words. "He doesn't talk about her."

The man's expression folded into sadness. "I suspect he has a lot on his mind."

Emotion burned along Olivia's throat. "What does he have on his mind, Papa Don? What has changed my father so much?"

Peppermints slid from the scoop into the little bag. With careful precision, Papa Don creased the top. "That'll be a nickel."

Olivia hesitated, the nickel clutched in her hand. She was confident that his hesitation, the same hesitation she'd seen in Marv, stemmed from a knowledge of something dark. "Please, Papa Don. I must know. Something is very wrong, and you know about it."

"Give your papa some time, Livy. Sometimes men need time."

Time? "This isn't about my mother's death. He's not a grieving man anymore."

"Maybe you coming home brings it all back." But there was a lack of conviction behind the words.

The door of the general store swung inward with force and bounced off the wall. "Don!"

Papa Don's gaze snapped to the visitor. Bobby Flagg stood there, his hat in his hands.

"Beg your pardon, ma'am."

"What is it, Bobby?" The storekeeper's gaze flicked to her then back to the foreman. His voice was a whisper. "Something's happened?"

"Found Hector Maiden. He's beat up pretty bad."

"No!"

The voice came from behind them. Josephine Laxalt came into view, her dark hair a direct contrast to the paleness of her skin. Her eyes went to Papa Don. "You see? They are dangerous. If we continue to resist, they will hurt us all."

Bobby Flagg pivoted and jammed his hat back on his head before he was through the door. Olivia had only a minute to make her decision. Her gaze went from Josephine's pale face to Papa Don's tense jawline and sober eyes.

"Tell me, Papa Don." Her words sliced the tense air between her and the older man. "Please stop hiding the truth from me."

The doctor arrived at the Maiden property just as Ryan stepped from Hector's house. He raised his hand to the gray-whiskered man with a large paunch and impossibly skinny legs. Only the presence of the clutch bag proved the man's occupation.

"Bobby's on his way in. He told me Hector's been laid low."

Ryan nodded and motioned the man into the house, not missing the frankly curious gaze the doctor speared at him.

"Name's Doc Herald. You must be Laxalt's boy. Heard you were in town."

Ryan's answer was to swing the door to Hector's room wide.

Doc Herald stepped inside and set his bag at the foot of Hector's bed. Ryan retreated a step.

"Could need some help. You've done a good job cleaning the wounds, but I'd like to roll him over and take a look."

"There's some gashes that need stitches," Ryan said from the doorway.

Doc Herald ran his fingers over the buckle of his leather bag. His gaze flicked over Ryan. "No need to be offish, I'm not one of the bad guys."

Ryan stilled. That was a strange choice of words.

"Your father was a good man. Didn't deserve what he got."

"What did he get, Doc? A bullet in the back?" It hadn't occurred to him until that moment how natural it would be for the doctor to have taken care of his father's body.

"I didn't see the deed done, son. They brought his body into town."

"They?"

"Your daddy's men. Your men now, I guess."

It lined up with what he'd been told by Bobby, except the part about his body being taken to the doctor.

"Was nothing I could have done," he said. His eyes narrowed as he tried to thread the needle in his hand. "Shot in the back. Went clean through the heart."

A wave of sickness welled in his stomach. He forced himself to relax and allow the tension to drain away. "Got any thoughts on who did it?"

Doc Herald lifted Hector's eyelid and picked up the threaded needle. "I've heard a lot of rumors. It's a serious charge to lay at anyone's feet."

"Seems to me the same name keeps coming up."

"Sattler? Yeah. But I wouldn't go poking a stick at that rattler. You might get a bullet in your back, too."

Was the doctor trying to warn him off? "They're picking the fight."

Herald's needle dipped into the gaping wound along Hector's cheek. "I'm not sure there's any defense."

Ryan turned away and pulled the door closed, unable to endure the conversation another minute.

"Hey!"

The door whipped inward, and the doctor stood there. His eyes flicked to the room beyond Ryan's shoulder. "Listen to me. Your father's dead because he tried to stop them," he whispered. "I'm not for anyone in this thing, but I don't want to be burying any more good men either. You want to win this, you'll have to band together. I've told them all that for months, and I think they're finally listening."

"Who worked Hector over?"

Doc Herald glanced back at his patient. His brows lowered. "My guess is Hector overstepped himself."

"We heard something last night when I was over here talking to him. Came out this morning to check on it. We didn't find anything."

"They're watching everyone. Probably saw you and decided to pick a fight."

"Framing me?"

"That'd be my guess."

"Sattler." Ryan hissed the word.

"Bowman and Michaels." The doctor's nostrils flared. "It's not just one of them, son. It's all of them together that's making things so tough."

Bobby Flagg walked in the house, sweat-streaked and dirty from the ride. But it was the slender, redheaded form that slipped by Bobby who stiffened Ryan's spine and made him feel like he was plunging off a cliff.

Chapter 21

"Couldn't get her to stay in town, boss." Bobby shrugged.

Olivia's head jerked around, and she plunged a hand to her hip. "It's not like I was asking permission. If I want to come and see Mr. Maiden, I'll come and see him."

"Check on Cody and Ty," Ryan said to Bobby. "I'll be down there as soon as I finish up with Miss Sattler."

Olivia sauntered closer, stopping two feet in front of him. She was covered with a thin layer of Wyoming dust, and her nose had a fresh sprinkle of freckles on a deep pink background.

"You've got sunburn." As soon as the words escaped, he wanted to groan in exasperation.

She rubbed at her nose and winced. "I didn't have a hat."

Staring down into her upturned face sent his senses reeling. What was this woman doing to him? She was pretty. Check. She was spunky. Check. She was maddening. Check. She was a Sattler. The enemy's daughter!

He spit his words. "We need to talk, Olivia."

"How is he?"

"He'll recover." She seemed so concerned. "They beat him pretty good, but nothing's broken that I could see."

"They?"

"I was with him this morning. All was fine that we could see."

Every word his mind formed jammed up in his throat. Watching her, those eyes… His heart squeezed in his chest. "I need to ride down to Ty and Cody. Find out if they've discovered any reason behind the attack on Hector." He was a fool. A coward in the face of a slip of a woman who balled him up inside so tight he had trouble drawing breath.

"I'll ride with you."

He gulped. "It's probably a better idea for you to—"

"We can talk."

Talk. Sure, he could do that. He'd listen while her lips moved and her eyes blinked and that little nose continued to get redder. He lifted his hand, intending to touch the tip of that sunburned nose, but he caught himself, embarrassed at the pull of impulse. "You can't continue to ride in this heat."

Her smile was a slow upward curve of pink lips that were at once teasing and amused. "You'll let me borrow yours, you being the kindhearted sort."

Ryan called himself every kind of idiot for letting Olivia Sattler get under his skin. The sight of her astride her horse with his hat flopping down around her ears took too much of his energy away from the problem of Hector Maiden's assault. He should never have allowed her to ride with him. He should have demanded that she stay behind and boil water, or do something, for Dr. Herald.

He slowed his horse to allow himself more time to survey the surroundings. He needed to look at the fencing and the crops for signs of intruders or stray prints, but everything around him faded away as he fell under the spell of watching her.

She twisted in the saddle and jabbed her index finger into the brim to tilt the hat away from her eyes.

Those eyes…

"Something wrong back there?"

Ryan shifted in the saddle and raised his head as if he'd

been searching the ground the whole time. "Everything looks fine."

"Does it?"

He glanced at her and caught the look she gave him and, again, that amused smile. He cleared his throat. "Cody and Ty probably have a lot to report." He leaned forward and squinted at the ground, looking for footprints, dung, marks of passage, anything that would mean he wouldn't have to look at her. To his dismay, he could feel the heat of a blush on the back of his neck.

"I think you're cute, too."

Her words snapped him upright. She appeared innocent sitting astride her horse. But that smile was back, and now she was laughing.

"I—" He cleared his throat to loosen the words wedged there.

"Right." She faced forward, the words falling over her shoulder. "You keep looking for sign. I'll ride ahead."

And with that, Olivia Sattler poked her horse in the sides with her boots and left him stewing in the Wyoming sun— and suffocating in the cloud of dust kicked up by her horse's hooves.

Olivia knew she shouldn't have goaded Ryan. Her comment had embarrassed him. She never would have guessed the deeply tanned cowboy with the dark hair and silver eyes was capable of blushing so nicely. In Philly the good-looking men had often been full of themselves. Even those with lower social standing were stodgy in manner—humility was never a part of their makeup. She realized now how distasteful that world had been. It was part of the reason she'd grown so restless to leave and come west. And now here she was, galloping on a horse in the middle of a pasture so wide, beneath a sky so blue, that she felt free and settled. This was home.

Or it would be home if not for the cloud over her head.

Her joy deflated. Papa Don and Josephine Laxalt knew

something. It seemed everyone knew something except her, but she'd had little time to beg the merchant for the full story. Riding to see Hector had taken primary concern.

She slowed her horse until Ryan caught up. He reined in the short-legged mustang that put her at eye level with him.

His expression seemed guarded. Tough. And she wanted so much to reach out and touch his arm and try to make sense of the emotions his presence stirred in her. But it wasn't the time, and he must think her terribly bold for what she'd said. Aunt Fawn would have had the apoplexy.

Her nose tingled, and she touched the tender spot. She'd known exactly what he'd wanted to do when he'd lifted his hand earlier, and the very idea had tripped the beat of her heart. But he had pulled back at the last minute, and she wondered if she'd repulsed him somehow. Maybe she was too forward or too—

"Are you feeling all right?"

She put a hand to her neck, mulling the question. The answer was a resounding no, but saying as much would bring more questions. "I saw your mother today. This morning, to be exact."

"Oh no."

His reaction stopped her cold. "Oh no?"

"She told you she's knitting booties?"

"Why…no. Baby booties?"

Ryan averted his face, but this time, this close, the stain of red on his neck was very noticeable.

"Is she making them for someone?"

"Forget I said anything." He closed his eyes and exhaled sharply. "Go on."

She leaned forward to stroke the horse's neck, her words coming fast. "Papa Don knows something about my father. There's more to all this than we're seeing, Ryan. I'm convinced of it. Marv said Tom Mahone wants me to write what he wants me to write. My father even suggested a few subjects for me to use for my articles. Then Papa Don seemed strange when

I started talking about my father. And then Bobby came in, and your mother started warning Papa Don that someone was going to get hurt. They know something, but no one wants to tell the whole story."

She blinked at the wetness that had gathered in her eyes. She hadn't meant to cry. It seemed such a silly thing to do. Olivia swiped at the tears and gasped at the friction of her hand on the tender, sunburned skin. She felt a warm bundle against the back of her hand and realized Ryan was offering his kerchief. She blotted the wetness and choked on a garbled sob.

"I don't know why I'm crying."

"Because you're hurt and confused. That would be my best guess."

She nodded at his assessment. When she faced him, her hat slid forward. He breached the distance between them and tilted it back on her head. His eyes smiled into hers. "Now could you say that all again a little slower?"

Chapter 22

Ryan listened to Olivia and tried his best to connect the dots. He wondered if she realized how much her heart showed in her face. Even the hurt when she talked of her father's remoteness.

He told Olivia what Dr. Herald had suggested. The similarities seemed too much to dismiss easily. "It's like everyone is watching the bully, but no one wants to help."

"Because they're afraid," Olivia said. Her voice was flat, resigned.

Ryan drew his mustang closer to the bay and reached across to touch the back of her hand. There was nothing he could offer in the way of comfort. Not until they knew more. "Let's go see what my men have found."

She nodded, and he withdrew, taking the reins and setting the pace. When Bobby came into view, the sheriff was with him. His small eyes were on Ryan as he drew closer. Ryan instantly disliked the man.

"Laxalt. Heard Martin's son had come back." He offered his hand. "Sheriff Bradley."

Ryan shook his hand and kept his expression neutral. He turned as Olivia stopped her horse and slid to the ground unaided.

"Who's this?" The sheriff jabbed a thumb Olivia's direction.

"Olivia Sattler."

"Sattler's girl?"

"It's not Sattler's boy." Ryan regretted the poke as soon as it left his mouth. No reason to rile the man. Bobby laughed and slapped his leg.

"Still the smart-mouthed kid I remember."

Ryan couldn't recall the man. He wondered if the sheriff's memory was faulty or if he'd just given ear to the rumors about his character based on the past and formed his own opinion.

"What have you found, Sheriff?" Ryan pressed.

"Your man here says he found the fence cut and was going to talk to Hector about it. Being that this section of the fence borders your property, it means you'd better put that smart mouth to doing some explaining."

Ryan had asked for that. He noted the myriad of hoofprints in the dust and weighed what he was seeing against what he wasn't seeing. "Aren't all our cattle bunched up for the drive, Bobby?"

"Just a few in this pasture. No more or less than last check."

Ryan turned his attention to the sheriff and raised his brows. "Why would I cut my own fence?"

"You tell me. Throw off suspicion. Hector have something you want? Maybe you're taking up where your daddy left off."

Bobby exploded. "That's a lie!"

Ryan raised his palm to soothe the foreman. "I can see where you're taking this, Sheriff. This isn't an investigation at all. You're acting as judge and jury."

"Makes perfect sense to me. You cut the fence then went to see Hector and did a little fist work on him. He's not a young man, which means you'd have the advantage. Your foreman already said you were out here this morning."

"You should look for someone with bruises on their face," Olivia said. "Ryan doesn't have a mark on him."

"On his face, Miss Sattler. Doesn't mean there aren't marks elsewhere, unless you…"

A hard edge of indignation propelled Ryan forward. He gripped the man's shirt and pulled him to his toes. "That was uncalled for, Sheriff. Miss Sattler is a lady, not that you would recognize one."

He felt Olivia's hand on his arm. "Ryan, let him go."

"Not until he apologizes."

The sheriff's face went red. Bobby moved up behind the sheriff. "I think the boss is right. No reason to insult the lady. Seems you're the one with the smart mouth."

Sheriff Bradley's eyes shifted to Olivia. "You have my apology."

"Louder," Ryan growled.

"You have my apology, Miss Sattler."

Ryan let go and took a broad step back. "Why don't you get on up to the cabin, Bradley? Sheriff's no good if he can't get the whole story before throwing insults and lynching an innocent man."

Bradley's scowl was ugly. "I'm telling you like I see it."

"Then maybe you'd better open those little eyes of yours and take a closer look. One based on fact. Hector and I talked last night and heard a commotion among his cows. We were investigating this morning to make sure all was well."

"Why did he need your help doing that?"

"He didn't. I came because I wanted to see for myself if he had found anything. You can't blame me for being cautious since my father was murdered."

"Murdered," Bradley spit. "That's your word."

"That's all the word you need."

The tense group moved toward Hector Maiden's house. They met Ty and Cody on the way back, and Bobby fell back with them. Olivia heard them whispering. No doubt Bobby was filling his men in on what had happened.

She rode close to Ryan, catching glimpses of him. She was worried that he might get caught in the middle of the mess.

"What if he's not awake?"

Ryan's chest lifted, and his breath exploded on the exhale. "Sheriff has his way, he'll probably hang me."

Olivia gripped the reins tighter in her right hand. "That's not funny."

"Wasn't trying to be funny."

"What if Hector can't remember anything?"

"Then I'm in big trouble unless we can figure out who did it. I don't think our sheriff is going to be much help."

"He doesn't know that you did it."

Ryan's eyes went over her, and a lazy grin broke the solemnity of his expression. "You don't know that I didn't."

She wanted to protest his statement, but a valid doubt niggled at her. She didn't know. Or did she… "In my heart, I know you didn't."

Ryan took a kerchief from his pocket, rolled it, and tied it around his neck. "Appreciate that, Livy."

Chapter 23

Hector woke up as the afternoon faded to evening and a chill rent the heat of the day. Ryan sat at his bedside, opposite Sheriff Bradley. He'd sent the hands back to the Lazy L and had tried to get Olivia to head home, but she'd given him a stubborn look, complete with hands on hips and sunburned nose tilted to the ceiling. He'd retreated.

Hector's bedroom was still redolent with the smell of the pork Olivia had fried up for supper when the man first showed signs of waking. Hector's grimace of pain became a groan.

Sheriff Bradley got to his feet and leaned over him. "Hector? You hear me?"

Hector's head moved back and forth against the thin pillow beneath his head.

Ryan went to the doorway, his footsteps alerting Olivia. "Hector needs a drink."

She nodded, and he returned in time to hear the sheriff's question.

"Who did this, Hector? We're needing to know."

"Take it easy," Ryan warned. "Let him get his head about him. Miss Sattler's getting a drink."

"I'm the sheriff." The older man scowled. "We're doing this my way, Laxalt. I'm not having any hired gun tell me how to do my work. Don't have any respect for a lawman who turns dark horse." He leaned forward as Hector's eyelids fluttered. "Hector?"

So he knew. Tension throbbed behind his eyes. He'd thought his reputation as a Ranger might help him; he should have known turning hired gun would erase all the good.

Ryan thought he heard a door shut. Feminine voices drifted to him. Ryan retraced his steps. He was surprised to see Phoebe huddled with Olivia. Phoebe saw him and waved him over.

"I came out here to warn you, Ryan. Sheriff Bradley is one of them." Phoebe's lips pursed as if she'd tasted something sour. "I had hoped you would leave town quick, but you haven't, and we all agree it's not fair for you to take up this fight alone, ignorant of the depth of the threat you're facing." She glanced between them. "Both of you."

Ryan digested the information. He felt the light weight of Olivia's hand on his arm.

"You're talking about Papa Don and Mrs. Laxalt?" Olivia asked.

Phoebe's eyes flashed. "There's more of us. Many more. We're all trying to band together, but they've got too much money and too many of the major players on their side."

"Sattler?" Ryan asked.

"Bowman and Michaels. All three of them." Phoebe nodded.

The weight of Olivia's hand shifted as she tightened her hold and swayed toward him. Her expression was pale and pinched with stress.

Ryan drew her up against his side. She molded into him. Phoebe placed a hand on her friend's shoulder. "I'm sorry. I was so excited to have you come back, but not to this. I had hoped your presence might…" Phoebe glanced away, clearly distressed.

"Who else is involved?" Olivia asked.

"Doc's on our side," Ryan said.

She tilted her face to his. "He told you that?"

"Just about. But he was vague."

Phoebe nodded. "We're a cautious bunch for a reason." She faced Olivia. "Tom Mahone is their puppet. He'll say anything they want him to say."

Olivia's face turned into his shoulder, her words muffled. "Why didn't you tell me that when I told you I was going to work for him?"

Olivia jerked back from Ryan, the fire of temper consuming her weakness. "I thought you were my friend."

Phoebe didn't meet her eyes. "How do you tell the daughter of the territory's biggest rancher that he's leading a band of killers? I tried to hint to you, thinking maybe you would go to him and have a talk. That having you home would soften him up some."

"He doesn't have time to talk. Not about things that don't matter to him."

"I used to work for your daddy, back when he was a loving father. But…people change. And I've watched him change over the years. It's as if the absence of your mother's gentle influence opened the floodgates to vileness."

Olivia shuddered with suppressed rage. "Did he kill Ryan's father?"

"There's no way to prove anything." Phoebe brushed at her riding skirt. "They work like that. No witnesses. No warning. Their men do a lot of the dirty work, especially Skinny. It's rumored that he's a hired gun from up north."

Questions sprang to her mind, but Olivia clamped down on the urge to ask them when Sheriff Bradley's raised voice hollered from the bedroom. "I know you're out there, Laxalt. Hector's saying some mighty interesting things about that temper of yours. Says you're good with your fists, too."

Ryan's inhale whispered in the silence. Olivia touched his shoulder, fearful of his reaction. "He's baiting you. Go back to town with Phoebe. I'll tell him you left. Send your mother over or Papa Don or Marv"—Olivia turned to Phoebe for help—"anyone who you know is on our side."

At first she thought her pleadings had fallen on deaf ears. She felt the knot of Ryan's muscles beneath her hand, and his dark eyes gleamed with anger then faded to frustration. Tension melted from his body.

"Ryan, listen to me. You can't go in there alone."

"She's right, Mr. Laxalt," Phoebe whispered. "Bradley will do whatever it takes to protect the big bosses. Even shoot you in cold blood."

His eyes rested on Olivia. "My men can keep the sheriff company and be witness to what Hector really says. I'd rather have you with me."

Chapter 24

Ryan hated leaving, even knowing that Bobby, Cody, and Ty would do everything they could to keep Hector safe from the sheriff. His horse kept pace with Phoebe's long-legged pinto and Olivia's bay. On the edge of Maiden's land, another rider moved out from behind a low hill and sat in their path. Ryan tensed, and his hand went to the scabbard that held his Marlin rifle. Phoebe glanced over at him and shook her head then waved at the man in their path. The stranger waved back.

Phoebe brought her horse up next to the man. Her mouth was moving before her horse had come to a full stop. "Ryan's men are with Hector."

Ryan worked his horse's pace down to a walk and pulled up between the man and Olivia, keeping his side to the stranger and his hand near the leather sheath that held the gun. Just in case.

"You must be Martin's son." The man nodded. "I imagine your presence has put some knots in Bowman's plans. Heard you were a Ranger."

Ryan shrugged, feeling no need to explain beyond that for now. "Something like that."

Phoebe turned to Olivia. Twin spots of color bloomed on

her cheeks. "Jacob and I changed our minds. We're going to get married." She laughed.

"Bowman's not too happy since the arrangement will give us more land," Jacob added, sharing a smile with Phoebe. "But we don't aim to make things easy."

Ryan tried to take in all the information that was being dumped on him, setting up the people who were the main players and those who were merely the puppets. Olivia didn't appear to be listening. Her eyes were on the ground as she unconsciously rubbed her horse's neck.

"Did the sheriff make a scene?" Jacob asked Phoebe.

She nodded over at Ryan. "Tried to pin the whole thing on him."

Ryan had a question of his own. "How did you know about Hector?"

"Word travels fast in a small town, Laxalt. Phoebe works at Landry's, so she can keep her ears sharp for rumors and accusations that Bowman, Sattler, or Michaels might be trying to churn up. It's how they've worked for years. Accuse the little man. Dispense with him and take over his property."

"How're they doing it? Setting up the scene? All those hoofprints…"

Jacob and Phoebe shared a look. Jacob shrugged. "Your pa was a good man. He saw what the big ranchers were trying to do, and he got vocal about it. Tried to figure out how they did it, too, but with the sheriff playing favorites, it's not like they need much more than a few hoofprints and a cut fence."

Phoebe guided her horse around his and over to Olivia. The two talked in low tones.

Jacob continued, "Him, Jon, and George tried to start their own paper arguing against the high price to register brands and the portable cabins the big ranchers are using to claim more property. George never had a chance. And there were threats against Jon. Anyone who stands in their way."

"George was killed?"

"An easy target because he was far out and a widower. No

witnesses. Same as Hector." Jacob glanced toward the women and lowered his voice. "I know Phoebe's been awful worried about Miss Sattler."

With all that had been revealed, Ryan knew Olivia must feel very much caught in the middle. Without her father, she had no family.

"Phoebe," Jacob called. "Let's get on into town. I think it's a good time to bring them into the circle. Papa Don has gotten everyone together."

Ryan tugged on the reins and fell back with Olivia. He wanted so much to reach out to her. He couldn't guess what she must be feeling and thinking. Though she had suspected her father's underhanded ways, to have them confirmed must be a terrible, heartbreaking shock.

He brought the mustang close to her mare and pulled his hat from his head. "Guess you don't need this now that the sun's not so high."

She barely raised her eyes.

"Livy?"

Her chin jerked up, and he saw her emotions contained in the sheen hazing her eyes.

"Maybe things aren't quite as bad as you think."

She averted her face, and he could see the moisture skid a streak down her cheek. "It's worse."

He reached out and touched the back of the hand that rested on her leg. "Does that mean you regret coming back? Even if it means you wouldn't have met a gentleman like myself?"

His try at humor fell short. She sniffed and pulled her hand away to wipe at her eyes. "I guess I just need some time."

He let it go, acknowledging his bad timing in delivering such a line. He was content to ride in silence beside her and used the time to form the questions he still wanted to ask of Phoebe and Jacob. To his surprise, they skirted Main Street and came up behind the Occidental and the other buildings before dismounting at Landry's. An outbuilding shielded them from any curious eyes that might be looking out of second-story windows. A man—or was it a boy? Ryan couldn't tell in the darkness—claimed each of the horses and led them into the shelter.

Olivia was at his side, hugging herself. "It might be better if I didn't go inside," she whispered. "I'm the enemy."

He clasped her hand in his and rubbed along her cold fingers with the pad of his thumb. "I won't go in without you. Whoever's in there must know you've been gone for so long there would be no way you could be a part of anything."

"You didn't."

"Because I've come to know you. They will, too, but you've got to give them that chance."

She cocked a brow. "You speaking from experience?"

He lifted his hand to her cheek. "Yes."

Her smile was fragile. "I'm afraid."

Ryan lifted his head to see Jacob entering the back door of the restaurant. Phoebe stood outside a moment longer, her face turned toward them.

"You're with me and Phoebe," he said. "There's no reason to be afraid."

Almost against her will, her right foot took a step forward. Ryan's hand on her arm urged her along, and before she knew it, she was in the back room of Landry's second floor living space staring open-mouthed at the familiar faces surrounding her.

Chapter 25

"It's not going to stop. When the governor repealed the Maverick Law, things really heated up."

"Maverick Law?" Olivia snapped the question. Her hand hovered over some papers. Ryan smiled. She was following his urging and taking notes of all that was being said about Bowman and Michaels, though he did notice that the Sattler name hadn't come up once. He could only attribute it to the group's deference to Olivia.

"Unbranded cattle become the property of the Wyoming Stock Growers Association," Papa Don explained. Based on what Olivia had overheard earlier, the storekeeper's presence hadn't been a surprise. Neither, for that matter, had Marv's. But Ryan's mother's presence, along with a half dozen men from small ranches on the other side of Hector Maiden's and west of town, had surprised him.

"It's to their benefit?"

"Yeah." Marv nodded. "We banded together to get it repealed. Wrote a dozen letters. Your daddy made the trip to talk to the governor himself."

"It's why he got shot." His mother spit the words then covered her face. Phoebe put her arm around the woman, and things grew quiet. Across from them, Ryan swallowed hard, feeling the weight of his father's sacrifice.

Marv cut through the silence. "Latest issue of the paper will feature Miss Sattler's article front page." He gave her an apologetic look. "Mahone's showboating the fact that a Sattler works for him."

"Did he try and run any more lies about us small ranchers?" a man Ryan had never seen before asked.

"Not much this issue," Marv acknowledged.

"It's their word against ours. You still sending those articles out to the papers in Sheridan and Casper?"

Marv nodded. "If anything happens, there'll be more than just us knowing our side." He stole a look at Olivia. "I didn't know what side you were on at first, but since you're here…" The man hesitated. "If you want to help us out and write about the injustices going on, I'll put them in the little paper me and his pa"—he bent a thumb at Ryan—"got started before them murderers killed him."

Olivia's gaze went to Ryan's.

He inclined his head to let her know the news did not surprise him.

"It's the principle of the thing. We have to get others to understand and fight." Landry finally cut through the silence. "They're doing their best to take land that doesn't belong to them. It's what George's death got 'em—and the burning of Tandry's cabin east of Bowman's range. Hector getting beat up wasn't a random act; it's a warning."

"Of what?" Ryan asked.

Landry swiped beads of sweat from his forehead with a meaty fist. "Hector filed for a brand. Cost was high, but he had to do it. If the brand isn't recognized…it's trouble. They rejected his petition, which makes anything carrying his brand illegal."

"Let me guess," Ryan spoke up. "They have their hand in the board that decides these things."

A man with a medium build and bright red hair spoke up.

"They can deliver fines and take the cattle, undoing the years it's taken a man to build his herd, not to mention wiping him out financially."

"That gives them a reason to beat him up, too. But why bother him? His herd of calves isn't even that large."

"They'll say he stole those calves. Beat him up to make a point with the rest of us—that they're winning." The red-headed man leaned an elbow on his knee. "They know you're around?"

"Yes," Ryan said.

"Then you can expect trouble."

"Sheriff's already fingering me for doing the deed."

Murmurs went up around the room.

"I left my men there."

"Expect more trouble when your men start the drive, and you're all alone."

"It's like I've said for months," Doc Herald's voice squeaked out, "if we don't band together, they'll crush us. One by one. This seems to indicate Hector is the new target."

Doc continued. "I'm sure he still wants the Laxalts. If he can put the blame from Hector's beating on young Laxalt here, then he's killing two birds—"

Josephine moaned and covered her face. Phoebe hugged the woman close.

"He's already trying to do just that. Which is why I left my men with him."

"I agree with Doc," the redhead said. "We've used every excuse for why we can't stand together. I know we're all pressed for time and money, but it's our only chance. I don't want another man's blood on my hands when there's something I can do to help. We need to set up a guard or patrol at Hector's until he can get back on his feet. He'll have to hire some help."

Conversation flowed around him, yet Ryan didn't hear a word of what was said. Instead, his mind was filled with Olivia. The sight of her. The scent of her hair for that brief moment he'd held her against his side outside Hector's cabin.

Her delicate freckles and the humor that lit her eyes and con-
founded him. As if she felt his gaze, she faced him. A deep
well of sadness etched her expression.

Ryan couldn't look away. She was beautiful on the outside, sure, but her spirit captured his interest—her ability to
stand for right even though it was her father in the wrong.
She'd been a friend to his mother, and his mother obviously
loved her already.

Across the space her eyes probed his for an answer to a
question he didn't quite comprehend. She raised her hand
to her hair, and his gaze followed the movement. Her finger caught a strand and twirled it around her index finger in
a nervous gesture. He breathed air into his lungs and wondered at the pull she had on him and what it could mean. She
lowered her hand, and the strand of hair bounced into place
beside her cheek. A brave smile curved her lips, reaching out
to encompass him.

And then he knew what had happened, what had shifted
within him, and understood the feelings her presence stirred.

Ryan Laxalt had a clear vision of what it all meant—he
was a doomed man.

Olivia was jostled and lost sight of Ryan as the crowd
shifted around her. Phoebe leaned close. "The meeting's
over." Her friend's voice held a distinctive smirk. "Not that
you noticed."

Pulled back to the present, Olivia felt the heat rush into her
cheeks. "I got distracted."

Phoebe patted her shoulder. "Of course you did."

Jacob stood in front of Phoebe, and her friend smiled and
placed her hand in his. The sight of Phoebe taking Jacob's
hand brought a swell of sadness. They wouldn't see each other
as much. Her world would become even lonelier. "Phoebe"—
she tugged on the back of her friend's riding skirt—"will we
see each other?"

"I'll be around. We can still visit."

Phoebe pulled her into a hug. A question rose in Olivia's mind that she had long wanted to ask of her friend. "Where's my mother buried?"

Phoebe flinched. "You...don't remember?"

"I remember a big tree and a mound of dirt beneath it. Daddy didn't let me stay there long."

Her friend's mouth opened then closed. "The tree... Your mother is...under the tree." Olivia didn't understand what she was seeing in Phoebe's expression. It wasn't a difficult question, or shouldn't have been. Her thoughts beat a warning tattoo.

Olivia felt a presence at her back and a hand against her elbow. She half turned toward Ryan, trying to make sense of Phoebe's struggle and the stab of fear it brought.

Jacob slipped a hand around Phoebe's waist, and the action seemed to give her strength and settle her panic. "Ask your father," Phoebe said. "He'll know."

Chapter 26

The red-haired man's name was Pete, and he told Ryan not to worry about Sheriff Bradley. "We'll be keeping an eye on Hector. Bradley talks big, mostly because he knows he's riding the big horse."

"You mean Bowman?" Ryan asked.

Pete spit into the tall grass and cleared his throat. "Bowman, Michaels, Sattler. Whoever waves the money at him. Pardon me, ma'am. Meant no disrespect."

Ryan sought and found Olivia's hand buried in the folds of her riding skirt. She gave Pete a vague smile before Ryan helped her into the wagon next to his mother. Both women were quiet, but Olivia's paleness had him most worried. He tied her horse behind the wagon his mother had brought into town. Olivia set the pace. Pete caught up to him astride his own horse.

"Heading your way. I'm west of town. It'll give us a few minutes to talk."

Ryan let the wagon move ahead to give them privacy to talk. "Did you set up guard for Hector?"

Pete tilted his head. "Didn't you hear us do that? My night's tomorrow."

He pursed his lips. "Guess my mind wandered."

"Your night's Monday." Pete scratched his chest and bobbed his head. "They'll probably target Isley next."

Ryan was incredulous. "Phoebe?"

"Yeah." Pete spit again. "Bowman wants Isley's land pretty bad. And the fact Jacob's marrying Phoebe and adding her proved-up section to his means there'll be trouble."

"Jacob's on guard?"

The red-haired man shrugged. "Sure. It's become a way of life."

He noticed for the first time the guns Pete was wearing. "You pack all the time?"

Pete nodded. "Good idea with so many snakes crawling around, if you get my drift."

A vague path shot off the main trail ahead. It would be the route Pete would take. Ryan berated himself for not paying closer attention during the meeting. He should have asked more questions.

"Reckon if you worked with the Rangers, it means you're a fair shot."

"Fair," Ryan said.

"We'll be glad for your help. Your daddy was a good man."

Hearing the words ripped open the grief again. It seared along his muscles and set his nerves to tingling. His father was a hero. Ryan was a killer. The burden of that bent him up on the inside. But there was no use wasting energy on his past right now. All he could do was take up the cause his father had championed and step into the empty boots his death had left behind. Maybe there would be some redemption in that.

Olivia could hear the whispered words of the men behind them. She wondered what they would talk about out of their earshot, and then thought it probably better if she didn't know.

"This is good," Josephine said. "Ryan getting to know these people will help protect him. I am sorry though, for you, my dear."

Olivia squeezed her eyes shut. "Me, too."

"Your father is not kind?"

"He is…distant."

The woman leaned close to her and planted a kiss on her cheek. "You are a good young woman. I would be pleased if you would let me remain your friend."

"I need all the friends I can get."

"This is good. Ryan will be your friend, too."

"He is, yes." Ryan's mention of baby booties slipped through her head and pulled a smile from her.

"I worry about him."

"He's smart. He'll be careful."

Josephine's eyes snapped to her. "Yes. Maybe now. Maybe for you."

Olivia's palms dampened, and she wiped them down her skirt. "I don't know about that. My father wouldn't be pleased to know we are friends." Did her feelings for Ryan and her friendship with Josephine put them at greater risk?

"This is nonsense. Your father is his own man, making his own decisions. Ryan sees that. I see that. I will not allow any man to dictate who I can and cannot befriend."

"Thank you, Josephine." The wagon rattled on. Olivia noted no other sounds of conversation from behind her. Pete must have taken the turnoff toward home. She wondered if Ryan could now hear their conversation.

"Will posting guards work, do you think?"

Before Olivia could form an opinion, Josephine answered her own question.

"We cannot know what works until something is first tried. I would give up the ranch if it meant keeping my son safe."

"What does he want?"

"To fight, as his father fought."

"You mean for the ranch?"

"Yes."

Olivia pulled on the reins to slow the team along a rocky section of the dirt road. In all her grief, she'd forgotten Josephine's. "I am sorry about your husband."

"My husband's death brought my son home. That is enough."

It must have been terrible for Josephine, those weeks before Ryan returned. To be alone and never know whether she would see her son again. In some ways, Olivia could understand all too well what the woman was feeling.

"Ryan is the type of man who could not live with himself if he did not try to find the man who killed his father."

"But then what?" Josephine's voice went high with strain. "When he finds that man, will he also kill to gain revenge? The beginning of blood spilt forms a long line of death."

She tried not to imagine Ryan holding a gun to her father's head. Pulling the trigger because their investigation led him back to Jay Sattler as his father's murderer. Olivia tasted Josephine's fear.

"The only hope for my son is to gain the attention of the law or walk away and leave this thing alone."

"But you were at the meeting tonight. Doesn't that mean you believe in what they are doing?"

"I want to help, but I do not agree that they should seek out trouble. Band together and try and find peace, yes."

Olivia saw it clearly then. Josephine blamed her husband for getting himself killed. While she could understand the woman's logic, she also could see Ryan's and the rest of the group's need to protect themselves against the pinch of the larger ranchers.

"He is a careful man. Not the angry young man who left here all those years ago."

Josephine gave a little grunt "I see he has told you much."

No, she wanted to say. She really didn't know much of the man Ryan had been, but she was learning the man he had become. And she wanted to learn more. Much more.

The wagon picked up speed on the smoother stretch of road. Sattler range was coming up. Olivia wondered if Skinny would be on watch, reporting to her father who his daughter was with.

"You can drop me at the edge of the property gate." Olivia pointed. "I'll walk."

"Yes. This would be for the best."

Olivia hoped Ryan wouldn't take it into his head to follow her to the door again.

When Olivia stopped the wagon at the edge of Sattler property, he straightened in the saddle. Olivia stepped to the ground and came to untie the bay. He saw her intent and gave the mustang a jab to catch up before she could get in the saddle and fade into the darkness.

"See your mother home, Ryan." Her voice shot out to him as she lifted the reins over the horse's head. "She's tired."

"My mother would be the first to chastise me for letting you walk in the dark alone."

"Ryan." She moved close to him and reached out to touch his leg. He could hear the pleading in her voice. It drew him. Soothed him. Without thought, he slipped to the ground, the saddle creaking beneath his weight. He faced her in the dark, the new moon wreathing her face. She had been so pale earlier. Stressed, no doubt, by the day's events.

"I'll ride beside you." He cupped his hands. The moonlight dimmed as the sphere slipped behind a cloud.

"I'm a liability, Ryan, don't you see that? I'm not fitting into my father's plans. If they see you, it gives them a reason to shoot first. If they see you with me, then it's an even better deal, because my father's rid of me."

He straightened. "It takes a cold man to kill his own daughter."

"He wouldn't have to be the one to pull the trigger."

"I don't believe he would order your death, Olivia. It's… inhuman. You're letting your emotions run wild."

He heard her sharp intake of breath as she hugged herself. He wished the moon would appear so he could see her face better, but it lurked behind the dark clouds that threatened rain but never followed through on the promise.

Ryan didn't know what to say. Her fear chilled him. She was just as vulnerable to her father's rejection as Phoebe had thought. He only wished her friend was here now to offer her female counsel. An idea skittered through his head.

"Come home with us."

He heard her gasp.

"My mother is there," he said, trying to deflect any immoral suggestion. "She can chaperone. I'll sleep in the bunkhouse." The silence embarrassed him.

"I would like that very much."

He heard a whisper of movement and saw the blur of her, like fog in the night. Her hands touched his shoulders, and he could feel the warmth of her close to his chest, her breath warm against his chin, then the softness of her lips on his cheek.

His heart raced, and he put out a hand to steady her. His fingers had only skimmed her waist when she stepped back into the darkness. His head spun with the quickness of her action and left him with a longing to feel her close to him again.

"You're sweet, Ryan. Let's see what your mother thinks first."

Chapter 27

Ryan could have told Olivia that his mother would exude happiness and light at the thought of having another woman around. What he didn't expect was the way the two chattered and laughed far into the night, as if all the cares of the evening held no weight. It was late. Late enough that he lifted the bundle of blankets and clothes he had gathered earlier and left the two sitting at the kitchen table. Olivia was listening intently to his mother's memories of her as a child. And of her mother.

He was eager to hear what Hector had said to his men about his assault. Surely with witnesses to the contrary, Sheriff Bradley would be forced to back off his accusation.

Bobby, Cody, and Ty were sound asleep, along with three other men who lined the rows in different positions of repose. Ty's snores vibrated the bed frame he'd crashed on, while Cody slept like a dead man, still and quiet. The grunts and coughs coming from the men hired for the drive brought back all the days he'd spent on the trail, gulping dust as he helped move cattle. He'd spent those wandering days realizing the painful reality that living means working, and that Martin Laxalt was a man who had only sought to bring his young son to understand and embrace the truth of it.

He stretched out on the last of the two unoccupied bunks

and laced his fingers behind his head. When he'd first come to Buffalo, he'd thought he would avenge his father's death and move on, but now there was Olivia. He closed his eyes to bring the vision of her face into full focus. He could see the flash of her eyes and felt again the feathery brush of her lips against his cheek. He raised his hand to touch the spot and smiled into the darkness; then he closed his eyes and fell into a deep sleep.

Olivia hadn't heard Ryan leave. She'd been unable to hide her disappointment at finding his bedroll gone from the space beside the front door. She would see him in the morning, she was sure, and the nighttime chat with Josephine had sharpened so many memories dulled by the passage of time. Exhaustion pulled at her, and she made the move to stand, smiling at the woman across from her. "I guess I'm more tired than I thought."

"Tomorrow is a good day for rest. A picnic. I baked bread this morning and can make bacon sandwiches."

"Picnic?"

"Of course. Saturday should not be all work."

"Where will we go?"

"To see Hector and take him bread, then out to the pasture beyond the hill. It is beautiful there." Josephine arched her back and stretched her arms. "The morning will be busy. We must cook for the hands. They leave on the cattle drive on Sunday. Monday at the latest."

She thought that might mean Ryan would be leaving as well. Her insides ached at the thought of yet another friend leaving. Her mother had always taught her that she was never alone. That God was always nearby. Even Aunt Fawn, in her own way, had sought to soothe her homesickness with promises of God's presence. It had brought her peace then; it could as well now. She smiled and covered Josephine's hand with her own.

"You can stay as long as you'd like, Olivia. You are welcome here." Josephine hesitated as wetness veiled her eyes. "I have always wanted a daughter, and you are like a daughter to me."

Olivia couldn't deny the draw of Josephine's words. Already God had answered the prayer of her heart.

Chapter 28

Ryan spent the morning with Bobby shoeing the extra horses. It was hot work that had them both soaked with sweat. When Ryan lowered the last hoof to the ground and stretched his aching back, Bobby swept him over to the chuckwagon for another check on progress. Bedrolls were already loaded, and the cook, Welt Ribbin, was stacking sacks of flour and beans. To Ryan's eye, Welt Ribbin looked older and more shriveled than a man of forty-nine should. Bobby must have seen his hesitation.

"Got him cheap."

"Hope it doesn't mean he's a terrible cook." Drives were hard enough without having to endure undercooked beans and burned bacon.

"Already tried him out. Makes the best biscuits I ever had."

Welt waggled his fingers, indicating Ryan should pass him another sack of beans. "I'll get 'em fed up and happy. Sleep like babies, they will."

Ryan raised the sack to the bed, and Welt dragged it over and stacked it.

"If'n you're done with me, I'll head over to the house and see if the womenfolk need some help. Teach them how to make some of my famous biscuits." Welt grinned and leaned so close Ryan could smell his fetid breath. "Not many women can make a good biscuit."

Amused at the man's audacity, Ryan kept his mouth shut. Soon enough Welt would figure out that Josephine Laxalt would rather be dragged by a horse through town than have a man in her kitchen. And especially a man who thought he could cook better than her.

"Should I have warned him?" he asked as they watched Welt waddle toward the house.

"Naw, your mama will have fun putting him in his place." Bobby lifted his hat and swiped at the sweat on his forehead. A frown mark folded a deep crease between his brows. "The men got to talking last night…"

Ryan leaned against the side of the wagon. "About?"

"Seems Cody and Ty are thinking one of us should stay. Help you guard the place."

"I can handle it."

Bobby gave a stiff nod. "Wasn't thinking you couldn't. Might keep the wolves at bay if they thought you and your mother weren't vulnerable."

Ryan stretched upright, his sore muscles protesting. "Like I said, I can handle it."

"As stubborn as your father."

He pushed off the wagon and lifted his nose. The acrid smell of burned hide filled the air.

"Almost done with the trail brand. Looked over Almanzo's herd yesterday. It's smaller than ours, but he's adding four men to the drive."

"More help will be a welcome thing for all involved."

"Ken's over at Hector's," Bobby said as he scattered the hot coals of the shoeing fire. "I'm headed over to relieve him."

"Ken?"

"One of the hires. Snagged him yesterday from a bar. Guess he was too scruffy for the big ranchers to notice."

"Is gathering hands always a problem?"

"Not until the big ranches got to hiring away our regulars. More money."

"Ken done a drive before?"

"Yeah. Up from Texas to Kansas."

"What brought him all the way out here and put him in a bar?"

"Drinking to forget, he says. Lost his woman giving birth to their son."

"The boy?"

Bobby shook his head.

"I want a clean trail, Bobby."

"I will, boss. No booze." The foreman stared hard over Ryan's shoulder, his jaw working. "I'm thinking the man needs a friend more than anything else."

Ryan could see where his father would have taken to the kindhearted foreman. That the man had a good eye for men also helped make him a good boss. A quality his father would have seen right away, just as his father seemed to see all the qualities a man was capable of, even if he never produced them. "Guess every man needs someone at some point."

"Sure, boss." Bobby lifted his hat and fanned the smoke. "That little Sattler gal wouldn't be such a bad friend."

Ryan glanced at his foreman, searching for any sign that Bobby meant disrespect. He saw only honesty in the man's weathered face, but he didn't want to answer the unspoken question and changed the subject. "Sheriff Bradley give you a hard time?"

Bobby shrugged. "Hector was talking just fine right before Ken got there. Never said one word about you beating him up, but he couldn't remember much either. That lump on his head might be the reason for that."

So the sheriff had been bluffing. No surprise. Ryan ground his teeth together, vexed by the dishonesty of a man who'd taken an oath to be upright in his dealings.

"The herd is smaller this year."

Ryan knew what that meant. "We'll pay the men what we owe and make do."

"Sounds like you might be planning to stay on permanent."

"What do you think Cody and Ty would say to that?"

Bobby's grin was huge. "They'd welcome it. We all would. Sattler would pick off the cattle one by one if he had to." The foreman shifted his weight and plucked the hat from his head as Cody and Ty came in from the corral. "Cook must not have gotten the boot from your mama's kitchen. He's waving at us to come eat."

They entered with the rest of the hands, bareheaded and polite in the company of the two women. Ryan noticed more than one curious glance at Olivia. She seemed oblivious to them all as she wore a path between the cookstove and the table, passing Josephine in the rush. Welt set a platter of biscuits on the table and took his seat at the end nearest to the kitchen.

"Your mama didn't like it too well, but I whipped up some biscuits and convinced her."

What Welt didn't see was the rolling of Josephine's eyes and the secret smile she shared with Olivia.

Ryan heaped a biscuit with jam and let the conversation flow around him. He offered a word here and there to keep things going, but his sole interest was in the woman folding squares of cloth on the other side of the kitchen. Her hair hung loose on her shoulders in soft waves that made his palms itch with the need to touch them. She turned, and he dropped his gaze. The last thing he needed was for her to get the wrong idea about his attention.

When Olivia refilled mugs of coffee, he found himself watching her all over again. He was mesmerized by the tiny smile she flicked at Welt as he passed her an empty platter. Then she was near Ryan's end of the table offering a refill on coffee. He nodded and held his cup. Her skirts rustled, and he did his best to ignore the sight of her slender hand holding the coffeepot. He fastened his eyes on Bobby and spouted some inane conversation he hoped made some sense. If Bobby noticed anything amiss, he didn't show it. Only when she returned to the cookstove was he able to draw an easy breath.

Bobby leaned forward and asked a question that made no sense to him. Something about pink bunnies and cancan skirts? But he trusted his foreman had asked a sensible question and it was only his hearing that couldn't make out the right words. He nodded at Bobby in answer.

Bobby reared back in his chair and barked a laugh.

Ryan scowled. The foreman leaned forward, and this time Ryan paid close attention.

"I thought she might have you distracted. I asked if you wanted to dress the horses in cancan skirts." He shook his head. "She's got you tied up tighter than a roped calf."

Bobby's tan face creased into a grin. Before he could form a proper retaliation, the foreman scooted his chair back and addressed the hands. "Let's get going, boys. We've got a long day before pulling out tomorrow." He ran a hand over his neck as he returned his attention to Ryan. "I'll take care of things, boss."

Ryan sat rooted to his spot as the men filed out. Maybe he'd change his mind and go out on the drive. But his mother tied his hands. He couldn't leave her, and when his gaze landed on Olivia, all thought of leaving became distasteful.

Olivia stacked plates, and he rose to take them from her. Her smile made his mouth go dry. His mother appeared, holding out a sack tied with hemp in one hand. She placed it on the table in front of Olivia. "Here you go."

"What's this?"

His mother's smile encompassed both him and Olivia, and those dark eyes shone with mischief. "A picnic lunch."

Olivia sputtered. "But I thought…"

Josephine half turned toward her. "I never said the picnic was for you and me."

Olivia blinked up at him.

Ryan didn't know what to say, but the idea of spending the day with Olivia… There was only one correct answer. "Thank you."

Chapter 29

"Your mother is quite the plotter," Olivia said. She tipped her chin toward the sunshine. It felt good to see her so at ease, but he knew Jay Sattler would not take kindly to his daughter lodging at the Laxalts'. He didn't know how she would react to the question, but it begged to be asked. "What about your father? He needs to know where you are."

Olivia scratched her cheek and touched the tip of her nose where he saw that the skin had begun to peel. "I'm going to move into town. Live in Phoebe's old apartment and work for Robert."

"Quitting the paper already?"

Her look was scathing. "You know Tom wouldn't print anything I wrote unless it was what he deemed acceptable. I'd rather write for Marv."

"He can't pay you."

"And I wouldn't want him to. It's my way of making up for whatever wrongs—"

"Don't do it to spite your father."

She sighed. "No. Your mother said the same thing, and I'm not."

"Are you going to tell him?"

"I will. Today. Later. I just want to think about it and make sure it's the right thing to do. To pray."

To pray. Ryan squinted into the morning sunshine. Maybe it was time for him to give God a chance. It would feel good to embrace something bigger than himself. And yet it was more than that, too. He'd heard enough from his mother to know her opinion on doing what was right when faced with choices. His most regretful choice had been condemning an innocent man before knowing the full truth. A mistake he determined with God's help not to make again.

His gut clenched as the familiar weight of guilt shifted against his conscience. He'd been wrong. Wrong to kill. Wrong to condemn without hearing both sides. It would be easy to excuse his behavior as shooting in self-defense, and he had, but he had also been determined to bring the man in to jail and collect his money whether the man was dead or alive.

The weight of his sin pressed harder. If only he could have a second chance. But he couldn't. He could only learn to be fair and patient. He squeezed his eyes shut. *I'm so sorry.* His throat thickened. *Help me be the man You want me to be. Fair. Honest. Hardworking.*

Olivia followed Ryan through narrow cuts and wide pastures. They rode for an hour by her best guess toward the Big Horns. It didn't seem to her that he was following any certain path but just meandering. She wanted to ask, but he seemed so deep in his thoughts.

Her own problems swirled thicker than the dust coating every stitch of her clothing. In the deep recesses of her mind, something Phoebe had said the previous evening bothered her, but the more she tried to focus on it, the further it slipped away. She wondered if Ryan had picked up on anything.

"Ryan?"

He reined his horse in closer, all attention on her. "Need to stop? It sure is hot."

She set aside her question and let him think that was going

to be her request. Besides, a rest would be good. Her hips ached from being in the saddle for so long. "I guess I need to do more riding."

"There's a stream up ahead. We'll stop there." His grin put a sparkle in his eyes that pulled her in. The angles of his face gave him a tough appearance, but his smile melted away the hard edges, and she could see more of the little-boy mischievousness that his mother had probably had her fill of when he was young. "It's the far corner of your father's property."

"I don't remember this part." That wasn't saying much, since her father's ranch was bigger than her nine-year-old body ever could have hoped to explore. But now, on horseback, she wanted to see it all.

East of them, the sun glinted off water. Nudges of the past came forward. She pointed. "Let's go there."

When they stopped in the shade and she knelt to drink, the need for rain became even more apparent. Tree branches arched over a very shallow pool, familiar somehow.

"It's not the best quality, but it's wet," Ryan said. He led the horses closer so they could drink. "I should have warned you to drink your fill before we left."

"I wish you would have."

The horses didn't hesitate to suck up the water.

She pulled off her hat and fanned herself. Ryan knelt at the edge of the water. His broad back hid his actions from her view, but when he faced her and held out his damp kerchief, she accepted it without hesitation.

"Press it to your neck. Like this."

He took it from her hand and refolded it into a long rectangle. "Now lay it across the back of your neck."

She lifted her hair with one hand and placed the cool rag along the hot skin. Ryan plucked the string from his hat and held it out. "As much as I love to see your hair down, better use this to tie it up. You'll be cooler."

Feeling like a child, she reached out to take the thin piece of leather. Aware that he was watching her, she lifted her hair, gathered it together, and looped the leather tie around her curls. She felt his eyes on her and marveled at how easily they had come to know each other. Things had changed between them since those first days, and she welcomed it. But even as she felt drawn to Ryan and thought he felt drawn to her, she worried what danger their relationship presented to him and his mother.

"We should eat. I'll need to check in with Bobby."

"I thought Bobby said he would take care of things."

Ryan glanced at her as he lifted the sack of food from his saddlebags. He fussed with the hemp, not looking at her. She allowed herself a little smile. Ryan Laxalt, she realized, was shy. If living in the city had taught her anything, it was socialization. Still, she should have seen that his quiet nature would align itself with shyness.

Olivia took a step closer. "Need help with that, cowpoke?"

He raised his eyes to hers and held it out. "Can't seem to get my fingers around that knot."

When her hand brushed against the bag, he withdrew as if touching her meant spreading cholera. "Ryan?"

He looked like a man trying hard not to show fear. "I'll get the blanket."

"Wait a minute."

He stopped and faced her.

"Don't you think it's time?"

A bead of sweat trickled down his cheek as she took another step closer. "For what?"

"To kiss me."

Chapter 30

She held out her hand to him. An offer. An invitation that he would be a fool to ignore. "Shouldn't we…I mean… Don't couples court first?"

"I'm open to that idea, too."

Ryan relaxed as laughter bubbled in his chest. She was so honest. She'd seen right through his excuse of eating so they could get back. He didn't want to go back, truth be told, but neither was he sure what to do with the feelings being near her stirred. He felt unsure of himself; having never been a ladies' man put him at a disadvantage. What did he have to talk about other than the ranch and his mother and the Wyoming heat?

He would be nothing like the men back east. Suave and mannerly in their crisp jackets with their fancy pocket watches and perfectly barbered hair.

"Ryan?" She took a step closer, and he felt choked by her nearness.

"Did you have a lot of admirers back east?"

Her brow knit. "You mean, did I have a beau?"

He gulped air and nodded.

"No. Though Aunt Fawn sure tried. The men were always worried about calling cards and proper dress." She made a face. "It's one of the reasons why I wanted to come back, though I didn't quite understand that until I was able to put away the fancy dresses and expensive hats."

"You don't miss it?"

"Ryan Laxalt." Humor glinted in her gaze. "What are you so worried about? That I have someone waiting for me back east?"

"No. More that you might not."

She shook her head. "I don't understand."

"If you did, that would end everything. But because you don't…" He reached out to cup her cheek, and she nestled her face against his hand. Though the light of her spirit beckoned him, the reality of who she was made him hesitate. He could not broach the subject in his heart without lancing the fester of another worry. "I want to do this right, Livy. No secrets."

Her smile dimmed. "Secrets?"

"Not mine, but the one we would have to keep from your father."

She pulled back. "We'll tell him then."

"Do you know the wrath we might suffer as a result? I have to think of my mother's safety, of our ranch."

Olivia presented her back to him.

"I'm sorry. It's as much a problem for me as it is for you." He wanted to continue that statement. To speak the truth he'd known to be true in his heart since that night at the meeting, but the words died before crossing his lips. Not here. Not in the shadow of her father's disapproval.

"Ryan…"

There was a tremor in her voice, but when she faced him, she raised a hand to point, a new alertness in her expression. "That tree. It's the one I remember. This pond… Daddy tied the horses up here, and we walked over to my mother's grave."

He lifted his eyes in the direction she pointed. A large bur oak stood, its massive branches each as big around as a sack of flour.

"Are you sure?"

"Yes," she breathed, a new excitement in her voice.

He took the lunch from her and tied it to the back of the mustang's saddle then gave her a hand up. They moved in unspoken agreement toward the spot. As they neared, the green crown appeared to rise out of the ground to show off its thick trunk. Yet Ryan saw no sign of a grave marker.

"Oaks are pretty common to this area." He tried to smooth over the obvious. "It could have been—"

"No. It was this one, Ryan. This tree—I'm sure of it. I remember the pond, the slow walk up here from the water, and the mountains framing the background."

He scanned the area farther out and glimpsed something through a thick copse of trees. "There's a cabin over there. If anyone's there, they might be able to tell you if there's a grave nearby." Ryan doubted it. A memory from when she was nine years old would be more than a little hazy. Surely. On the other hand, if she was at the grave of her mother, wouldn't it have made an indelible impression?

To him the cabin didn't look very old. Nothing moved, but there was a curious mix of spring flowers blooming in the front. A rose grew in wild abandon at the corner of the house. Greenery would have withered by now in the drought, yet the rose's green leaves made Ryan cautious. Someone had watered the rose—daily, by the looks of it. The flowers in the front were healthier closer to the bush, recipients of the runoff, no doubt.

Olivia galloped her mare to the place and slipped to the ground before he could caution her. She ran to the front door and pounded her small fist against the wood.

Ryan scanned the cabin and thought he saw the slightest movement at a tiny window. He left the horse to cross to Olivia as she pounded again. A scuffling sound came from within and then a scream.

Chapter 31

Olivia's fingers curled around Ryan's arm. The horror of that high-pitched scream jolted through her body. When the door suddenly swung open, a pale-faced woman glared at her then over her shoulder at Ryan.

"What do you want?" She turned to look behind her, shifting her body as if to block the view. "Mr. Sattler send you here with the food?"

"I'm sorry." Olivia's voice snagged the woman's attention away from Ryan. The matron stared, eyes narrowed. A slow dawning understanding twisted her expression a second before she slammed the door.

Olivia turned away, shaken and confused.

"Livy?"

Ryan placed his hand on her shoulder.

From inside the cabin they could hear the woman's raised voice calling out to someone. Nothing made sense, not the woman's reception or her reaction or...

Olivia caught movement out of the corner of her eye at the same time Ryan's hand on her shoulder gripped harder. She turned to see a woman standing there. Her curly hair, gray at the temples, was smoothed back and held by two combs. And her face...

"Olivia." Ryan breathed her name.

The woman giggled, arms wrapped around herself. "I sneak out the back door sometimes. Agnes never remembers to lock it." She tilted her head in a childish way. "Are you my little girl?"

Ryan held on to Olivia's shoulder, bracing her up. The resemblance between the two women had struck him at once, and the sickening truth presented itself the moment the woman asked that question.

Olivia half turned to him, and he pulled her back against him, sharing his strength with her. Agnes flung open the front door and gasped when she saw the childlike woman.

"Lily, you shouldn't be out here bothering these people."

Olivia seemed to come alive and broke free of his grasp. "Mama?"

Agnes moved to block Olivia's advance. "Listen, child." Her voice became softer, placating. "Listen to me. It's not what you think. Go home. Talk to your father. Please."

"I want to talk to my mother."

"I can't let you do that." Agnes raised her voice; her tone was firm. "Go inside now, Lily." She spoke over her shoulder. "You're not safe out here."

Ryan curled his arm around Olivia's waist and pulled her away from the woman. With one last backward glance at them, Agnes followed Lily inside.

Olivia seemed dazed. No tears. No hysterics. Nothing. He turned her toward him. "Olivia?"

"Mama." Her little-girl voice rocked his spirit.

He ran his hand over her springy curls. He was afraid to speak for fear of making the situation worse with what he could only speculate. He held her close; his hand cupped the back of her head, and her face was buried against his shoulder. Ryan rocked her as they stood, wishing he could absorb the emotions pummeling her mind and heart.

* * *

Shock waves pulsed along Olivia's nerves. She felt on fire
with disbelief. The enormity of all she'd just experienced.
Her mother…

Alive.

Olivia closed her eyes. Ryan's arms were protective and
warm when she felt so cold and hollow. Phoebe's stricken look
as Olivia had asked about her mother's grave burst into her
mind and crumbled her emotions further. Phoebe had known.
She was sure of it. Bile burned in Olivia's throat. How many
others knew? One after another the questions rolled through
her mind.

"Livy…"

Ryan's rough whisper was filled with concern.

"You're shaking. Are you cold?"

She nodded against his shirt, and he massaged her arms,
trying to bring warmth into her skin. She felt cocooned in a
white haze where no thought penetrated and nothing mattered.
She felt herself lifted, carried, and she was going to shut her
eyes against the bright light…the sun? But the light persisted.
Only the wall of warmth at her back seemed real. Then she
blinked and understood that she was on the mustang. Ryan
was behind her with his arm securing her in place, and they
were galloping. Trees blurred by, and the heat beat down on
her bare head. Ryan shifted behind her, and the heat lessened.

He stopped, and she watched uncomprehendingly as he
knelt and lifted something. Then he was beside her again, and
she felt the saddle shift as he mounted behind her. His rough
fingers plucked at the neck of her dress, and a coolness lay
there that brought out the shivers all the more.

"Lean against me, Livy. I'll get you home."

Home.

The word echoed strangely through her mind, disjointed,
not a part of her or who she was. She pitched forward on a
sob, but his strong arm kept her from falling.

"Livy." His voice broke, a pleading whisper against her
ear, and then nothing.

Chapter 32

Olivia's mother ran to her, arms outstretched. Lillian Sattler whispered cheerfully against her nine-year-old ear. The sun shone down on their shoulders as Lily embraced her daughter and filled her in on the trip into town. Her words were a blur in Livy's mind, but her mother's skirt scratched against her cheek, and her hand was warm as she cradled Livy's face for a kiss then pulled out a small sack of peppermints.

Olivia's velvet slumber became the backdrop against which other long-forgotten scenes flashed. Smells. Her mother's golden bread slathered with jam. Lily's white apron. Tiny stitches that marked the passage of her mother's needle along the seams of Livy's favorite green dress. And underscoring all of it, the smell of peppermint... .

"Olivia?"

She opened her eyes, fully expecting to see her mother, but the scent dissipated and the face had dark eyebrows and hair. Kind eyes and gentle hands. She recalled the rasp of a voice against her ear, of warm arms lifting her, but not this woman's voice or arms. It was a man's... .

"Mrs. Laxalt." She breathed the word. "Ryan?" She closed her eyes, trying to piece it all together. Her mother's voice but not her mother at all. It had been the voice of a childlike waif; only the face was that of her mother.

Josephine lifted a cool cloth to Olivia's forehead. "Stay quiet. Sleep. Ryan went for the doctor. I've never seen him more worried than he was over you."

"Mama?"

Josephine went still, staring down at her in a strange way. "I'm not your mother." Her soft hand stroked Olivia's cheek. "Though I would dearly enjoy the privilege."

Olivia felt the stream of wetness streak her cheek. She was unable to find the words to clarify the miscommunication, and she wasn't sure she had the energy anyway. Josephine's words were enough, like a warm blanket on a cold winter night. She would wait for Ryan to return. She stiffened in fear.

"What is it, child?"

"Ryan's coming back, isn't he?"

"Yes my baby. He'll bring the doctor."

Fear exploded in her chest, and she turned her head aside. A sob escaped, followed by another. Josephine leaned in close and slipped her arms around Livy's shoulders. She lifted her to a sitting position, where Olivia let her tears fall in a daze of hurt and confusion.

"I'm here, Livy. I'm here."

Her throat throbbed with the fierceness of her crying and the rawness of wounds ripped open by a dose of harsh reality.

Every beat of the mustang's hooves was synchronized with the pounding of Ryan's heart. He had felt Olivia's despair and seen the evidence of her confusion as he'd rushed her to the only place he could think to take her—back to his mother. He knew his mother's love for Olivia would be a succor.

Anger burned like a hot coal in his gut. Jay Sattler had known his wife was alive. He'd sent Olivia off thinking her mother dead. Cold reasoning nudged at him with the truth. If Livy's mother had fallen into a stupor of unconsciousness and woken with her mind weakened, perhaps Jay had meant only to spare his daughter the distress. That he had shipped Olivia east made perfect sense in light of the truth, but it didn't excuse the man from not telling his grown daughter upon her return. Did he truly think she would never find out? She at least deserved to know the truth as an adult and be given the chance to deal with it in her own way.

His thoughts shifted back and forth as he rode, oblivious to the scenery. Only the beating of the horse's hooves and the need to get back to Olivia seemed real. He wanted to hold her close, feel her breath against his cheek, stare into those whiskey eyes, and know for himself she would endure the shock. They would face it together. He would bring in Jay Sattler and demand that the man talk to his daughter and help her understand why he had done what he had.

In the heat of the day, Buffalo was a lazy town. Ryan didn't see anyone. When he found the doctor's office empty, he went first to the Occidental across the street, then to Landry's, hoping to find the man at lunch. Robert Landry himself was waiting on the two patrons present in the dining room.

"What can I get for you, Laxalt?"

"Looking for the doctor."

Robert's meaty fist swiped along his shirtfront. "He's out." The man's eyes slid toward the back of the room then fastened on Ryan again. "Got that bridle you were asking for out in the barn if you want to look at it. Not giving it to you cheap though."

Ryan opened his mouth to protest then caught the meaning of Robert's words and actions. He sidestepped the man. "I'll take a look at it."

Together they went through the back door and out into the shack behind the restaurant. Robert shut the door as Ryan struck a match and lit a lantern.

"Heard this morning that Bowman found some of his stock gone. He's accusing Jacob and Phoebe of rustling his cattle. Apparently Jacob went after Bowman and took some lead for it. Doc's over there now."

"They find evidence?"

"Sheriff Bradley doesn't need evidence. You know that. He just needs the big boys to line his pocket with money."

"How'd you hear?"

"Pete came in for the doc." He ran his hands down his aproned waist. "You got an emergency?"

Ryan squeezed his eyes shut and rubbed at the space between his eyebrows where all his tension seemed to be settling. "Went out for a ride this morning. Found a cabin back in the woods on Sattler's property. Olivia wanted—"

"You were out riding with Olivia?"

"She asked Phoebe about her mother's grave."

Robert's nostrils flared, and he spit an oath.

"You know then?"

"Everyone knows."

"Then why didn't anyone have the guts to tell her? Do you know what it did to her to stumble upon her mother living out in the middle of nowhere, guarded like a criminal?"

Robert's hand clamped down on his shoulder. "You've got to understand. Sattler's in control. It's his secret, and the whole town knows about it. If one of us told it and he found out, do you think for a minute he wouldn't take out his revenge?"

"Isn't he doing that anyway?"

The big man's hand fell away, and his expression went bland. "Yeah. I guess he is." His words were soft. "Agnes is a good woman. She's paid well to guard Lily."

"You seen her lately?"

"Lily?" He shook his head. "No. Never. One of Sattler's men picks up supplies to take out there."

Ryan's mind tracked Robert's words closely. The inflection changed when he talked about Agnes. "You know Agnes pretty well?"

Robert's eyes snapped to his. "About once a month she comes to town for supper."

"Doesn't anyone question that? Who she is? Why they never see her."

Again Landry shook his head, his expression pained. "No. She's my wife."

Chapter 33

Robert Landry shared everything then. The reason he was both indebted to Sattler and appalled by what the land barons were doing to the little men. "I thought I'd have to close the restaurant, but Sattler offered to help me out. We went way back, so I didn't think a thing about it. But he confided that Lily had become too much for Phoebe, and he needed some one else. He asked Agnes if she would do it, and she agreed. The money was good. It helped us stay open when the Occidental would have put us out of business."

"That's it? You're content never to see your wife? No one wonders where she is or what she's doing?"

"Rumor was she was going a couple towns over to help her invalid mother. Jay must have started it. How could we dispute that without backing ourselves into a corner? But eventually people figured things out."

"How about Olivia?" Tendrils of temper made him curl his fingers into fists. "What about the little girl who was sent away thinking her mother was dead?"

Robert's brows lowered. "You think I haven't thought of that? But what's the alternative? She finds out her mother is crazy?"

"Well, she found out anyway." Ryan spit the words.

"If anyone can help her through this, you can, Laxalt."

A dust devil swirled down Main Street then petered out as Ryan directed his horse away from Landry's. Everyone in town, even those at the meeting last night, wallowed in their fear of Bowman, Michaels, and Sattler. Despite the agreement that they needed to take more action and the effort to protect Hector as he healed, it wasn't going to be enough. Ryan felt sure of that now.

As much as he wanted to head back to Olivia, he couldn't. In spite of the secret Phoebe had kept from Olivia, the woman had been a friend. He didn't agree with the way she'd handled things, but neither did he agree with Robert, and there was no changing any of it now. What he could do was counter the sheriff's casual disregard for upholding justice, and he would have to do it alone.

Following Robert's directions, Ryan headed out of town the same way he'd come in, at a fast gallop. If Jacob Isley was laid low by a bullet, he would head out there to check on the situation, let the doctor know of Olivia's need, and help Phoebe keep Sheriff Bradley in line.

The face of his father loomed in Ryan's mind, and he thought Martin Laxalt just might be smiling.

Olivia woke with a start. Josephine's hand stilled her and smoothed her hair back.

"What time is it?" she mumbled, noting the shadowed light in the window.

"It's getting on suppertime. Are you hungry, child?"

All Olivia could think of were the bacon sandwiches that never got eaten, of Agnes standing in the doorway then slamming the door in their faces, and of her mother's frail silhouette and her singsong voice.

"My mother is alive."

Josephine's dark eyes glittered. "Ryan said something about you finding your mother. Do you want to talk about it?"

"Where's Ryan?"

Josephine stood up from her chair and stared out the window. "I don't know. He should have been back by now. He was pretty upset, and I suspect a lot of his anger is focused on your father."

She understood at once what Josephine feared. That her son would try and take on her father and end up getting shot.

"He loves you, you know." Josephine turned, a small smile on her lips. "I've never seen him like this."

Olivia didn't know what to say, so she said nothing. He was late returning, and Josephine's fears were becoming hers. She pulled herself to a sitting position, and energy flowed into her limbs. If nothing else, she needed to make good on her promise to tell her father of her intentions to move into town and work at Landry's, but what she wanted more than anything was the whole story about her mother. To know why he had chosen to keep her mother's life a secret. Had her mental state embarrassed him? She could not leave her mother alone, not now that she knew the truth.

She shifted and swung her legs to the floor. Josephine pulled the chair away from the bed.

"Are you sure you're feeling better?"

"I need to go to my father." Josephine's hand guided her to her feet. "Did you know my mother was alive?"

Ryan's mother shook her head. "I knew only what you were led to believe, that she had been sick and died."

Satisfied, Olivia smoothed her skirt, frowning at the wrinkles. "If Ryan returns with the doctor, tell him I'll be back, but please, please don't tell him where I went. Not yet."

"He will know."

It was true. She had already told him earlier that she had plans to talk to her father. After finding her mother, it would be the most logical conclusion to explain her absence.

Olivia put her hands on Josephine's elbows and squeezed. "Then if he's bent on coming after me, make sure he has a gun."

Chapter 34

Doc Herald shook his head as he came out of Jacob Isley's room, mad through and through, if Ryan was any judge of the man's expression.

"Who shot him?"

Doc Herald slumped into a chair and crossed his arms. "Never could get a straight answer out of anyone. Phoebe says it was the sheriff. I believe her more than the others put together. Bunch of lowdown snakes, if you want my opinion on the matter."

Ryan scratched his cheek. "Where is she?"

"Sheriff has her down at the place where he found the so-called evidence."

He pushed away from the table he'd been leaning on. "I'm headed there then."

"Be ready for anything, Laxalt. They're getting bolder."

"Because we haven't been shoving back hard enough."

Doc's eyes lit with amusement. "Do some shoving then."

"It's about time, I think."

With his hand on the door, Ryan turned. "You know anything about Lily Sattler's condition?"

Guilt spread over the doctor's face, and he dropped his gaze. "She was a sick woman."

"She's alive, Doc, and you know it. You the one who treated her?"

The doctor sat up. "Sattler knew something wasn't quite right. She'd had a fever that raged for days. Terrible. I did all I could to get it to come down, but… Then she slipped into unconsciousness. When she finally came around, she wasn't the same."

"Her mind went."

Doc nodded. "Jay took it hard. Mighty hard. He justified telling Olivia her mother was dead because it was true, to a point."

Ryan's grip tightened on the smooth wood beneath the pads of his fingers. "Olivia found out today. We found the cabin back in the woods."

"Oh my—"

"It was like it shattered something inside her. I rode into town to get you."

Doc was shaking his head. "Where is she?"

"I left her with my mother."

"Best place for her. She's strong. For any girl to take a stand against her own father, that's saying a lot." Doc scooted around in the chair and stood. "I've done about all I can for Jacob. Might be a good idea for me to go with you down there."

Ryan appreciated the man's offer. "Come on then." He turned toward the mustang and pulled his Marlin rifle from the saddle. "You might need this."

The sun had begun to sink when Olivia reached her father's house, bathing the yard and house in a rosy glow. No one came out to question her arrival or ask about her absence. The hands must have still been out on the range. She lifted her booted foot and took the last step to the front door of the home she'd been raised in. Her father had to have had a reason for what he did, muddled though it might have been by the grief he'd surely felt over her mother's sickness. Olivia inhaled deeply and raised her hand to knock. The pressure of her fist unlatched the door, and it swung inward with a low moan. But no one was holding the door.

The bare wooden floor creaked, and she jerked back. She stood still, straining to hear movement, and hugged herself against the chill of her stretched-tight nerves. Pulled by memories, she went to the section of the pantry where her mother's apron hung. Tears burned her eyes as she stroked the familiar material. She'd come for answers, yet maybe she'd been wrong. If her father would not answer her questions, the woman with her mother would surely know something.

She took the apron down off the peg and went out to the front porch where she settled into an old rocker. She would give her father some time before she went to Agnes. If he wouldn't answer her questions, she would at least confront him about his dealings with the other cattle barons. She should have done so long ago. If Ryan arrived, she would do her best to bring the three of them together and work peace into the relationship, and maybe, just maybe, her father could learn to accept Ryan.

And Ryan. He wanted to do things the right way and tell her father of their plans to court. She would honor that, and if her father didn't open up to her on the matters weighing on her mind, then she would move forward with her plans to live and work in town. And if Ryan Laxalt was part of that future—she smiled—then she would welcome his love and companionship.

The sun set over the dry land, leaving a vast expanse of pale sky fading to dark gray in its wake. She knew it wouldn't be long before her father came home. She gathered the apron close. She would wait; she had time.

Chapter 35

Sheriff Bradley struck an authoritative pose as Ryan and Doc Herald drew rein on their horses. All around the man and his companion, a bedraggled Skinny Bonnet, were hoofprints. Sharp edges of cut wire winked at Ryan as he swung down. Phoebe sat on a rock not far from the area in question.

"What do you want, Laxalt?"

Things would not go well, Ryan knew, but he was determined to keep things civil until he could take a closer look at the ground. Doc stood silently a little behind him.

"Since Jacob can't look at the evidence himself, Doc and I decided we'd be his eyes and ears."

"This is evidence. You can't come closer."

Phoebe stood and blinked as if dazed. She lurched forward then broke toward them. Doc Herald took a step in her direction and reached to steady her when she stumbled. "You should be at the house with Jacob," the doctor told the woman.

"I had to come. He wouldn't believe me." She shook her head, and her eyes welled with tears. "It's not fair. Jacob didn't even do anything." Her gaze swung to Ryan, and he felt the weight of duty being placed squarely on his shoulders.

His gaze went to Skinny's dusty boots then the dark scowl on the foreman's face. "That evidence you want to protect so much… Seems to me Sattler's man has already been allowed the privilege to examine it."

"I'm working for Bowman on this." Skinny sneered. "I'm an investigator."

"I think it's time we hire ourselves an investigator who doesn't have a stake in the big ranches."

Bradley's expression tightened. "I don't like the sound of what you're saying."

"And I don't like a sheriff who can't give a man a fair shake at defending himself before he starts shooting."

"Seems we're even then."

The sheriff's smile was cold, and Ryan understood how the man would think such a thing. "I learned from my mistake, Bradley. That's the difference between us. It's why I didn't kill Sattler right off."

"You sure didn't give Stephens a chance. You collected your money though, didn't you?"

"And I took it back when I discovered the truth."

"That doesn't make Stephens alive again. It just means you're a hotheaded killer."

There would be no convincing the sheriff of anything. "You would understand that last part better than most."

Bradley's lips twisted. "Jacob had it coming."

Phoebe took a step forward, eyes blazing. "That's not true—" Ryan held out his hand to block her momentum and halt her protest. She blinked at him, confused.

"Trust me," he whispered.

She gave a reluctant nod. Ryan swung his attention to the foreman then to the sheriff, who had positioned himself between Ryan and the area in question. Skinny Bonnet hadn't moved a muscle. Strange behavior for a man so bent on action. Stranger still that the man hadn't offered more than the sneering reprimand.

"Watch that Bonnet," Doc Herald said close to Ryan's ear. "He's poison."

"That's why I gave you the rifle."

Doc blanched and glanced at the weapon in his hands. "Should have told you, I'm not one for shootin'."

"Hard times call for hard decisions, Doc. If you can't do it, hand it off to Phoebe. She'd be delighted to put some holes in the sheriff's hide about now."

Ryan took a deliberate step forward then another. The sheriff flinched and glanced over his shoulder at Skinny. Ryan ignored both men and skimmed along the dusty, hoofprint-laden ground. "How many head?"

"Thirty," the sheriff bit out.

"Doesn't look like prints enough for that many."

"You callin' me a liar, Laxalt?"

"No." Ryan let the word settle. His eyes flicked to Skinny. "I'm calling Bonnet a liar."

Bonnet's angular jaw tightened. His faded eyes were pale as a rattler. His hand hovered over his gun, and Ryan held his breath. He was sure the man's stillness, his lack of appetite for violence, had less to do with the rifle in Doc Herald's hand and more to do with the boots on his feet.

It was simple, really, Ryan knew. And it heralded back to a case he'd worked for the Rangers to expose a group of rustlers. "Not going to draw, Bonnet? Most men would shoot me dead for such a thing. Especially those with a quick temper."

Skinny opened his mouth and spewed a stream of vileness.

Ryan let himself smile. "My mother would make sure you spent a day and night locked in the outhouse for such talk."

"Wait till it's just you and me, Laxalt. Just you and me on a hot day, and I'll be watching the buzzards pick your eyes out."

"So why don't you move over here, and we'll settle it. These good people can be our witnesses."

Out of the corner of his eye, Ryan caught the sheriff pivoting toward him. He turned to meet the blow and used his forearm to deflect the punch. It was the bark of the Marlin that stilled the sheriff. His slit eyes rounded with wonder and shock. He staggered back and clutched his midsection.

"You're not hit, Bradley. Doc couldn't hit the side of a

barn." Ryan swiped the sweat from his upper lip and kicked the sheriff's gun along the ground and toward Phoebe. "But don't take a swing at a man when he holds all the cards."

Bradley sputtered and straightened. "I don't know what you're talking about."

"Sure you do. That's the reason why you tried to crack me along the head." Ryan knelt in the dirt and measured the length of the hoofprints, following their path with his eyes. Behind him he heard Phoebe's sharp intake of breath and knew she, too, understood where he was going with his words.

"Looks to me like Mr. Bonnet is rooted to the spot." He stood and rubbed his jaw. "For good reason, too. Doc, why don't you hand that rifle to Phoebe and take Skinny's guns."

Skinny's face twisted. His hand flashed downward, but the rifle barked again, and the shot twisted Skinny backward and to the left. He didn't move.

Sheriff Bradley grunted and glared. His face ashen.

"Now." Phoebe's voice cracked like a shot. "I suggest you stay right where you are, Sheriff. At least until Ryan's had himself a chance to check out the bottoms of Mr. Bonnet's boots."

Jay Sattler moved from the shadow of the night and into the fingers of light flickering from the lantern Olivia had lit. His beard shaded his jaw and hid his mouth, but his eyes, vacant, hurt, told a tale of despair. He had transformed into an old man as soon as Olivia had invited him to the porch and told him she had found her mother.

"It didn't have to be this way, Daddy." Her heart squeezed tighter with each word.

He stared out into the night. "Were you with Laxalt last night?"

"Is that all you care about?"

"It's enough." His voice came heavy. "You think I want my daughter taking up with a Laxalt?"

"You mean 'the enemy,' don't you? But he's your enemy,

not mine. I have no ties to this land, remember? You made sure of that when you sent me east."

"I didn't want you to know… ." He cracked his knuckles, and Olivia saw his struggle. "It all came out wrong."

"You told me she was dead and watched me grieve."

He jerked toward her. "It was better that way. Don't you see? You would have rather had a mother who was crazy?"

"Yes."

"You wouldn't have, Livy. Believe me. You say that now that you're an adult, but as a nine-year-old, it would have shattered you."

She couldn't say anything. He had made the decision for her all those years ago, and what was done was done. "You were ashamed of her?"

Her father didn't answer for long minutes. The night breeze swept through, hot and dry, perfuming the air with the scent of dust and cattle dung—a smell Olivia would always associate with this moment.

Her father lowered his chin to his chest, and she heard his sharp intake of breath. The sound should have softened her, but she could think of nothing but her mother stuck in that cabin, of her nine-year-old grief, and most of all, of the man she had known as her father who had turned into a stranger with decayed morals.

"I wanted her to be well. Can you understand that? I thought that getting her away to a new place would help. Be less stressful on her mind and help her to heal. But it never helped. Nothing helped." His chest rose. "All I wanted was my family."

"Then why did you send me away?"

"Your mother…everything…it was too much. I couldn't think." He clamped his hands onto the railing. "What do I know about raising a girl? It was too much, and then Fawn offered."

"She knew?" Olivia felt a new wave of anger. This one directed at her aunt.

"No, of course not. She wanted to take you and give you the training you needed to be a lady, and I thought it was what your mother would have wanted."

"You know it wasn't. I would have been happier here. All the time I was in Philadelphia I felt like an outsider, and you never wrote."

"What was there for me to say, Olivia? Could you have handled the truth? Did you want to know what it felt like to—" He collected himself and squeezed his eyes shut, fingers pressed against the lids. Her own throat burned with the honest answers to his questions.

"It was ripping me apart inside. And I knew"—his hands fell to his side, and his eyes were red with trace emotion—"I knew I had to protect you from the pain of the reality. She doesn't know who I am. Didn't remember you or me or... anyone here. She thinks I'm just some nice man who delivers supplies and likes to listen to her talk." His chest heaved.

Olivia stood. The coldness she'd felt for her father was melting.

"I touch her, and she screams. Like I'm a stranger, a madman come to torment her or hurt her." He choked, and his voice was thick as his breath caught.

Her mother's change was killing her father, had been killing him for all the years she'd been gone. If nothing else, it was still clear that he cared for her, needed her to be whole. But Lily was unable to do so. The knowledge tore at Olivia and stirred her sympathy to new heights.

"Was it the fever?" she asked.

Jay shrugged. "Doc says it happens sometimes. The body recovers, but the mind gets stuck in the past." His lips pursed, and he stared up at the moon. "Lily loves to talk about her childhood. She has vivid memories of her parents and her dog." He closed his eyes, and his fists clenched.

"When I heard you were coming back, I didn't know what to do. It was so much easier to let things stay as they were."

Chapter 36

Olivia hugged herself. She wasn't quite willing to move to her father. Too many unanswered questions needed explanations.

"I've heard rumors."

Jay glanced at her. "It was what I feared, that others would tell you before I could find the courage to do so."

"No," she corrected, gathering her courage. Olivia was anxious that the shift in subject would shut down the line of communication. "No Daddy. I meant rumors about Martin Laxalt. About cattle rustling and…and…"

His mouth hardened.

"I wanted so much for it all not to be true, but the more I see, the more I hear…"

"It's that Laxalt boy. He's putting things in your head."

That her father could harden so fast to what she had to say was a mental punch.

"His father is dead, Daddy. I think he has a right to know what happened."

"Simple. Martin was rustling my cattle."

"Who told you that?"

Jay glared at her then stared off into the night. Her heart

sank at the implication of the silence. But the fact that he stayed on the porch at all gave her hope.

"Daddy, please."

"Skinny's in charge of the men. One of them saw the cut fence and the hoofprints. What's this young man to you, Livy?"

"I love him."

Jay's eyes drilled into her. "I didn't pull the trigger if that's what you want to know. Laxalt got testy about the whole thing and pulled a gun. Skinny shot him out of self-defense." His shoulders slumped, and he hooked a boot around the bottom rail of the fence.

"Doc says he was shot in the back."

"Then he's lying!"

"Or your foreman is."

A minute passed in silence; then her father's mouth firmed. "You love him?"

"Ryan's a good man."

Jay laughed, a humorless sound. "My daughter loves the son of a thief."

His eyes cut to hers.

"He's not a thief, Daddy. Martin Laxalt was trying to get some of the restrictions lifted on brands. He's a hero to many."

"How do you know that? Been listening to them, haven't you? Small ranchers who invade our territory and steal our land."

"What happened to you thinking of them as neighbors? Men with the same hopes and dreams as you once had."

Jay stiffened. "I guess we all know where those hopes and dreams got me."

It was a bitter statement. Olivia glimpsed the hard shell her father surrounded himself with rather than dealing with painful things. "I have dreams, Daddy. Do you want to hear them?"

Jay Sattler's boots echoed along the porch to the front door. "Are you coming in for the night, or are you headed over to Laxalt's again?"

The accusation in his eyes made her head spin. She averted her face, pained by the rejection.

Ryan shut his eyes for a moment and swayed in the saddle. He stretched, feeling the weariness of the mustang as it cantered toward home. Doc Herald followed close on his heels.

"You staying awake, Laxalt?"

Ryan suppressed a groan. "Don't want to be. But, yeah, I am."

"What you did back there..."

He didn't want to talk about it. Doc had tried numerous times to express his awe at the discovery of Skinny Bonnet's boots and the odd but effective wedge of wood with the hoof-print in relief on the soles.

"When I finally understood the direction of your thoughts, it was amazing."

Ryan shrugged. "Bonnet got sloppy. He wasn't measuring off his steps to resemble a cow's stride."

"And you got that all because he kept so still?"

Doc was unfamiliar with anything related to cows. Still, everyone had their gifts. He remained quiet as the horses went down a hill, their hooves churning dust. They were almost to the turnoff to Sattler ranch. He was tempted to take the route and roust Sattler from sleep to tell him of Skinny Bonnet's and Sheriff Bradley's fall from grace. Only his concern for Olivia kept him heading west toward home. Doc said something else, but it was lost as Ryan increased pressure on the mustang's sides and the animal put distance between them.

In mere hours, Bobby would be rousting the men, and they would start the drive. Ryan allowed himself a small grin. Without Skinny on the loose and the sheriff to back up every bad deed, perhaps small ranchers would have a greater chance at the next roundup. But that was a year away.

Ryan slid to the ground in front of the house and leaned against the mustang for a minute to collect himself. With heavy limbs, he released the saddle's cinch and lifted it from the mustang's back, returning for the saddle blanket and bridle. A slap to the rump, and the horse gladly trotted into the corral. Doc pulled in at that point. He was blissfully silent as he tied his horse out front.

Ryan motioned for the man to follow, noting the light beaming through the panes of glass before he opened the door. His mother sat at the table, as he knew she would, but he didn't expect the lines of worry around her mouth or the words that she spoke.

"She's not here, Ryan. She went to her daddy's and hasn't come back."

His head fell back, and he released a heavy sigh.

"Looks like my services aren't needed after all," Doc murmured, and clutched his black bag. "I told you your mama's care was the best thing for her. Now I'm headed back to get some sleep." He turned at the door. "You've got yourself quite a son, Mrs. Laxalt. A chip off the old block."

"You're exhausted," his mother said. "She is a smart woman, son. She will not dare ride through the night alone."

Ryan paced along the wood floor, grateful his mother did not probe for details about the doctor's pronouncement. But she was wrong about one thing. Olivia. There had been too many times when she'd tried to ride out alone at night, determined to get wherever she was going. And he knew something his mother didn't. If news got to Sattler of Skinny Bonnet's death and the sheriff's fall at his hand, Sattler would retaliate. Kill his cattle. Stage a rustling during the drive. Play his trump card and forbid Olivia from seeing him. Even now he could have formulated a plan to exact revenge.

"Drink this."

His mother pulled on his arm and directed him to the table. She pointed at a cup of coffee.

"You are just like your father, debating a problem when there is no solution to be had."

Torn by indecision, Ryan sipped at the brew. His mind was

rocking with images of Olivia on horseback at night, falling to the ground—as delirious and unfocused as she'd been after seeing her mother.

His mother's hand weighted his shoulder. "Ryan..."

He pushed back the chair and lunged to his feet. Her hand slid away. "I'm going after her. There's too much at stake. It could mean losing everything."

"The cattle?"

Ryan half turned toward his mother. "The cattle are the least of my worries."

Chapter 37

Tears stung Olivia's eyes as she held the apron close to her cheek. Sleep would not come, and every one of Ryan's warnings about riding alone at night kept her in place. She turned over on her bed and considered undressing and slipping between the covers, but the sound of hoofbeats coming fast stopped her.

She knelt at the window. Footsteps from the direction of her father's room told her he had heard the commotion as well. Her heart pounded in fear. If it was Ryan, what would her father's reaction be? Or Ryan's? She could see him being angry over what her father had done to her mother. Angry for her sake. She stood and strained to see through the darkness. It wasn't Ryan. She sagged against the wall in relief.

"What is it?" Jay Sattler's voice broke through the night sounds.

"Trouble." She heard the stranger's hiss. "Skinny was shot and killed. Laxalt—"

"Hush," Jay shot out. "Come inside."

She wanted to follow the conversation but knew that her father would retreat to his office for that very reason. Ryan was involved. Her heart sank at the notion that he might be hurt or followed, that even now her father could plot a way to bring Ryan to heel for whatever trouble he had caused.

Olivia plucked the apron up off the bed. She smoothed her hand over the material and mouthed a prayer, grasping for a thought that would make what she should do clear to her. *Lord, what now? What can I do?*

Ryan would not kill unless he was threatened. He was that sort of man. His father had been honorable. But she also knew his temper could rage hot. A specter of doubt inserted itself into her mind.

The inactivity would drive her mad. She bounced to her feet and stuffed the apron beneath her unsullied pillow. A tap on the glass froze her in place, and a face appeared at the window. Dark hair and silver eyes.

Ryan.

She gasped with a hand to her throat, at once afraid and relieved.

He put a finger to his lips and motioned her outside. She knelt inside by the open window. Their faces were inches apart. "I can't."

"Is your father holding you?"

"No. But I'm afraid for you. For Hector and—"

He jerked his head toward the hitching post. "Whose horse?"

"I don't know."

Ryan seemed to consider that. "Something happened tonight. Sheriff Bradley's going to get taken in by the marshal. Skinny Bonnet was the one staging the ground to look like cows had been rustled at Jacob's ranch."

"Jacob? You mean Phoebe's Jacob?"

"It happened tonight. Earlier. Jacob was shot, and that was where the doc was. Olivia?" Ryan's hand touched hers, and she started at the feel of his fingers against her. Her eyes snapped to his.

"What are you afraid of?" The tears came then. Ryan brushed them from her cheeks. "Come outside."

She sat on the sill and twisted. He pulled her through the window and supported her until she could get her feet under her. When he turned her in his arms, she saw in his eyes not a reflection of her own desires but the love and devotion he'd yet to put into words.

She framed his face, needing to hear the words locked deep inside him. They would dispel her doubts and remove the tarnish her father's veiled accusation had placed on her decision to stay at the Laxalts'.

He drew a breath, and his chest swelled. He held her close and searched her face, her eyes. His exhale washed over her.

"Ryan…"

"I love you, Olivia."

"We've got to get out of here."

"No."

"What if he comes after you?"

"Listen to me. Things are much different now. Your father no longer has the sheriff to back him, and Skinny was their hired gun." His hand stroked down her arm. "I have to face your father, Livy. For us."

She knew he was right. As much as she wanted to escape and be done, they would never live in peace until this thing between the Sattlers and Laxalts was finished. And Jay Sattler held the key.

He'd wanted to kiss away the trails marking her cheeks. But he could not bring himself to ply her with stolen kisses on the front porch of her father's house, considering the ill will between their families.

He stroked her hair, unable to find words to express his hesitation so that she would understand. Or maybe she did understand. "You need to go back inside and get some sleep."

She nodded against his chest. "We talked. Him and me. About my mother. I understand now, but…"

Her head sank down as the last word tumbled from her lips. He absorbed the silence, giving her the time she needed. He gauged the vague sound of voices coming through the window that allowed them the time for a stolen moment. When her silence stretched longer than he could endure, he lifted her face.

"Tell me."

"I tried to help him see that what he was doing was wrong. What he was allowing. Your father…everything."

He traced the curve of her ear with his finger. His father's face bloomed in his mind along with the words of his favorite phrase, and he heard himself repeating it. "A wise man once told me that what you can't work out, you can pray out."

Her hands tightened on his arms. "Do you believe that?"

A deep sadness rose in him. "I didn't, but I'm beginning to."

As if on cue, the heavy thud of boots on the wood floor beat out a warning. She pulled away, balancing on the window sill and twisting through the opening. He turned away and rounded the corner where the angle of the house, even with the moon shining down, kept his cowhand in shadow.

He raised his hand as Cody shook his head to indicate he had seen or heard nothing new since their arrival. Ryan jerked his head and went to the corner of the house, glancing around to watch as a single man exited, gathered the reins of his horse, and turned the animal. The dim profile wasn't one Ryan recognized, but he had an idea by the flashes of silver on the bridle and saddle that it might be Bowman or Michaels, and he wished mightily he could have heard what was said in the impromptu meeting.

Cody sidled up beside him, brow raised. Ryan nodded. As Ryan rushed to his horse, he knew his hand would settle in for the night, just as they'd planned. Someone needed to keep an eye on Sattler, and Ryan's command, above all else, had been for Cody to protect Olivia if she needed it.

Chapter 38

Ryan worked through the night alongside Bobby. There was a fever pitch of activity so the drive could get a head start if there was going to be trouble.

"Take 'em out of here, Bobby." He gave the signal to his foreman. Bobby raised the handkerchief around his nose and mouth, and the other men followed suit. It was the official sign for the hands to start moving the cattle. The indignant moos almost drowned out his words as the ground vibrated beneath the onslaught of hooves.

"Things will go well," his mother said. A cloud of dust rose into a dense ball as the cattle bunched together and picked up speed. "God knows we have had much to handle."

Ryan didn't respond. His mother's words echoed through his mind more as a prayer. The early start would give Bobby extra time to make six miles before resting and finishing with another seven or eight for the day.

"It's time for me to face Sattler."

"What about Olivia?"

The question stirred his doubts. She'd obviously been distressed at her father's refusal to change his ways, though seemingly touched by Sattler's explanation of Lily. Finding the strength to stand against her father would be a hard test of her loyalty and love. Surely she knew that if Jay Sattler could not be turned, her association with Ryan—or any of the small ranchers—would mean a rift in the father-daughter relationship.

In the wake of her emotions, his declaration of love had seemed the right thing to do. He would not take the words back. He just hoped he hadn't been premature, that the light in her eyes would not fade under the test to come.

Her father's back seemed an indomitable wall as he sat sipping coffee from his favorite tin mug. Olivia tied on her mother's apron, prepared to stand her ground against her father's preconceived notions of how Lily should be cared for. She fingered the edge of the apron, drawing strength from the familiar item.

"I see you stayed last night."

She firmed her lips as his statement flared through her. "You've grown suspicious of your daughter's morals?" She strained to keep her tone light, matter-of-fact instead of challenging. "Isn't the hope I would develop good morals part of the reason you sent me to Aunt Fawn and that fancy school?"

Jay sighed into his coffee cup. "One thing you have learned is the art of debate. Your mother could fashion a rebuke with a soft word, but it always came through loud and clear."

Vestiges of the broken emotions he'd shown the previous night showed in the faraway look in his eyes and the sad turn of his lips.

Olivia sat across the table from him—the same place her mother had occupied all those years ago. "I want mother to live with me." She kept her eyes on the table, wading out deeper into the pool of her desires. "Being out there all alone… I think it might be good to have her around people again."

"Olivia…"

"It's important to me to try and help her as much as I can, Daddy. Don't you see that? Did I tell you what she asked me as soon as she saw me? She asked if I was her little girl. She recognized me." Not until she felt the tickle on her cheek did she realize she was crying. She swept back the moisture and met her father's eyes, letting him see her determination.

"And what does your Mr. Laxalt think of that?"

His mention of Ryan made her cautious. "He's not 'mine.' "

"Weren't you defending him?" His tone was accusatory. "Trying to make peace between our families so you could marry him?"

Olivia clasped her hands in her lap. "Josephine Laxalt has become my friend—"

"You want me to believe you're doing it for his mother?"

"Let me finish, Daddy."

Jay opened his mouth then lifted his mug and took a long pull.

She took a deep breath and continued. "They're all my friends—"

The mug slammed down, making her jump. "Do you know what your friends did last night, Livy? They murdered an innocent man."

"Innocent in whose eyes?"

Her father's eyes narrowed. "What do you know of all this?"

"Enough to know there is another side to the story."

He stroked a hand down his beard and cracked the knuckles on his right hand. "Whose side am I hearing? Laxalt's? Did he come visit you last night right here under my roof?"

Olivia rose to her feet. She was shaking with fury. "There was a time when I had a father who was caring and kind and loving. Who would hear a man out before he condemned him. Whose heart was bigger than his ranch and who delighted in the idea of having and being a good neighbor. What happened to that man, because he doesn't live here anymore. If you know where he is, Daddy"—the sob rose in her throat and burst out—"if you know where he is, let me know. I'd love to talk and laugh with him again." She plucked at the knots of the apron and swept it from her body as she rushed across the room.

"Livy! Livy, come back here—"

She didn't stop until she got to the corral where a hand saw her running. She smeared the tears away. "Please, saddle up the mare."

"Yes ma'am, Miss Sattler."

Olivia glanced over her shoulder, waiting, almost hoping, that her father would appear, beckon her back, and wrap her in his arms. But the door didn't open, and she was soon riding into the early-morning wind.

Chapter 39

The sun was high in the sky when Ryan wiped his neck with the kerchief and adjusted his hat. It had taken all morning to break the pretty little mare, and his mind had begun to wander from the task, a dangerous thing when on the back of a bucking horse. He opened the gate and gave the mare a slap on the rump to send her off into the pasture to graze.

No sign of Olivia. No sign of Sattler, and he wondered after Cody, too. The man must be hungry by now, and he hadn't given specific instructions to the hand other than to watch over Olivia and report on strange activity among Sattler and his men.

His mother appeared on the porch and raised her hand. He thought she was shading her eyes until she extended her arm. A lone rider was coming from the direction of Buffalo and Sattler's ranch. The silhouette didn't match that of Olivia, nor did the dark horse seem familiar. Whoever it was must know they were giving him plenty of time to collect his guns, and that meant the person came without ill intentions.

"It's Jay Sattler." His mother's voice sounded breathless. Her dark eyes filled with worry.

"Go inside. Leave this to me."

"I'll go inside, but that rifle will be keeping me company."

Ryan put his arm around his mother, amused by her spirit "You do that." He leaned to pick up a stick, took out his knife and relaxed on the step.

When Jay Sattler brought his horse to a stop right in front of the step where Ryan sat whittling on a stick, he angled his hat to get a better view of the man. "Good afternoon, neighbor. Light and sit."

If Jay wanted trouble, nothing in his body language gave hint of it. "Olivia went off this morning. Thought she might be here."

"Haven't seen her."

Ryan rose to his feet as Jay advanced. "She's all I've got, Laxalt. And you...you've turned her against me."

"You come to talk or to accuse? Because if it's the latter, I've got my own accusation to level."

"I didn't shoot your pa if that's what's got you riled."

The confession came so swift Ryan felt his breath leave him in a rush. "Then you must know who did."

"Reckon you plugged him already."

Skinny Bonnet. "Who ordered it?"

Jay swallowed and frowned. "Now that would be telling."

Fury ate at Ryan's calmness.

"You've got my daughter all twisted up inside. Her loyalty should be to her father."

"Her loyalty, Sattler, should be to the side she chooses to believe."

"You killed a man."

"It wasn't my shot that put Bonnet in the dust. If there's any question of his innocence, then we kept his boots as evidence. When the marshal rounds up Bradley, we'll hand all that over."

"Just you remember that my hands are clean. I don't want no trouble."

"But you'll be glad to give trouble to others."

Jay's jaw went hard. "I just want what's mine."

Ryan gripped his knife tighter. "When a man proves up a claim, it's his. That's the law. You can't take land or what's found on it just because you think you have a right to it." He forced himself to relax. "You started somewhere. Why can't you give that chance to others?"

Jay stared toward the horizon. "Things change."

"Things change people—for the better or for the worse. My father thought you were a good man. A good neighbor. What happened?"

"This from a hotheaded kid who went off on his own? Who're you to give me life lessons?"

"I'm the son that wouldn't listen, who pulled a knife on his father because I felt he was making me work too hard. I'm not proud of that, and I've never forgotten it, but I have learned from it." Ryan felt a weight lift from his shoulders, as if giving voice to his past wrongs was a cleansing. "And there are other things, too. Things life has taught me about morals and fairness."

He saw Jay's gaze shift and felt a presence at his side. His mother's hand held on to his arm. "I am sorry about Lily, Jay. I'd like to visit her sometime. Maybe I can help her do the needlework she was once so fond of."

The man's lips trembled, and his eyes reddened. He spun away and stomped back to his horse then stopped, reins in hand. "That's right kind of you, ma'am." He grunted into the saddle but sat still. The horse pranced a bit. "Laxalt."

Ryan met his eyes.

"You find Livy. Tell her—" His voice caught. "Make her happy."

Chapter 40

When the wagon crested the hill and the cabin came into full view, Ryan caught sight of Olivia and Lily sitting side by side at the edge of the pond, their hands clasped together.

"It's like a ghost," his mother whispered. "After all these years, to find out Lily was here all the time. No wonder that poor girl was so devastated."

Olivia heard the rattle of the wagon before Lily did. He could see the smile on her face even from the distance that still separated them. He'd been headed out on the mustang when he'd crossed Cody's path coming in. He learned from the cowhand that he'd followed Olivia out to a cabin. Ryan had known right away where Olivia had gone and the reason. He'd returned for his mother and to exchange the horse for a wagon while his mother gave Cody supper.

"She looks happy," his mother said.

He didn't know if she spoke of Olivia or Lily, but both women did look happy. If only Jay Sattler could see his women together. When he brought the wagon to a halt, he took the bag from his mother and helped her down.

Olivia guided Lily toward them. The younger woman looked paler than normal. She seemed tired but happy.

"This is your neighbor, Mother, Mrs. Josephine Laxalt."

Lily tilted her head, and her smile revealed a dimple. Her skin was smooth and pale. "Have you come to be a friend to me?"

"I have. This is my son. He's a special friend of Olivia's."

Lily giggled. "I have a special friend, too. He comes to visit me sometimes."

Ryan heard Olivia's gasp. "Yes, a tall man with a red beard?"

Another giggle. "Yes. He tells me I'm pretty, and he brings me peppermints."

Olivia's eyes filled, and she stared out over the shallow pond.

"Why don't you two take a walk while I show Lily what's in my bag?" Josephine suggested. She opened the bag wide, and Lily looked down inside. "Do you know how to use these?" Josephine asked.

Ryan turned toward Olivia and touched her arm.

She fell into step with him. His chest tightened when they were alone. "Tell me what just happened back there."

"She recognizes my father. He said it had taken her years to let him get close." She stopped. "There's so much to tell you, Ryan."

He opened his mouth. "We'll have time for it later." The pond shimmered. It was a peaceful place. "Your father said you ran off."

She gasped. Stopped. Reached out to clasp his arm. "Ryan?"

"He came for a visit."

Fear crept into her eyes.

"It's not what you think."

Her breathing eased along with her grip on his arm.

"Livy." He released her hold on him and held her hand in his. He was afraid of the answer to the question he needed to ask. "Your father thinks you should be loyal to him."

"I'm sure he does, but you know I can't, Ryan." Her lip

trembled, and she bit it. "I think mother's illness shattered something deep inside him."

"Then maybe we can help bring him back to the light."

"I don't know. He's gotten so hard."

"We'll work it out. Little by little the Lord will guide us along the way." He held her shoulders and smiled into her eyes. "Can you believe that?"

She nodded.

He sucked in the warm air and raised his hand to her cheek, then touched the tip of her sunburned nose. "Your father told me something right before he left. We didn't agree on much, but on this we did." Her eyes were round with curiosity. "He told me to find you. To make you happy."

Her eyes were luminous, and a veil of tears bore out her relief. "Oh Ryan."

"There's more." He held her chin and brought her hand up to his chest. His heart raced. "Could you care for me, Olivia? A Laxalt?"

She took a step closer. "I love you, if that's what you're asking."

"I want to court you. Proper-like. Long rides. We could come out here to be with your mother. Whatever you want."

"Cowboy style."

He laughed and took in her eyes, the curl of her lashes, and the brightness of her cheeks and nose. "What more do I have to do to take care of you?"

"You could buy me a hat that fits."

Her soft smile encouraged him. His finger traced along her lips, and he leaned forward to kiss the sunburned freckles on her nose. She moved closer and tilted her head. He lowered his lips to hers.

A laugh echoed across the water to them and shattered the moment. He turned to see his mother and Lily watching them closely. His mother was holding up a ball of yarn. Something was tied to it that looked like...

Olivia's eyes went wide. "A baby booty?"

Ryan pulled her back into his embrace and kissed her nose before releasing a laugh. "Or we could just fast-forward to the wedding."

* * * * *